# THE SCIENCE OF LOST FUTURES

## WINNER OF THE BOA SHORT FICTION PRIZE

# THE SCIENCE OF LOST FUTURES

## STORIES BY RYAN HABERMEYER

### WINNER OF THE BOA SHORT FICTION PRIZE

AMERICAN READER SERIES. NO. 30

BOA EDITIONS. LTD. ❖ ROCHESTER. NY ❖ 2018

First Edition
18  19  20  21    7  6  5  4  3  2  1

For information about permission to reuse any material from this book, please contact The Permissions Company at www.permissionscompany.com or e-mail permdude@gmail.com.

Publications by BOA Editions, Ltd.—a not-for-profit corpo-  ration under section 501 (c) (3) of the United States Internal Revenue Code—are made possible with funds from a variety of sources, including public funds from the Literature Pro- gram of the National Endowment for the Arts; the New York State Council on the Arts, a state agency; and the County of Monroe, NY. Private funding sources include the Lannan Foundation for support of the Lannan Translations Selection Series; the Max and Marian Farash Charitable Foundation; the Mary S. Mulligan Charitable Trust; the Rochester Area Community Foundation; the Steeple-Jack Fund; the Ames-Amzalak Memorial Trust in memory of Henry Ames, Semon Amzalak, and Dan Amzalak; and contributions from many individuals na- tionwide. See Colophon on page 216 for special individual acknowledgments.

Cover Art: "'you're really talented,' she says" by Andrew Rice
Cover Design: Daphne Morrissey
Interior Design and Composition: Richard Foerster
Manufacturing: McNaughton & Gunn
BOA Logo: Mirko

Library of Congress Cataloging-in-Publication Data

Names: Habermeyer, Ryan, author.
Title: The science of lost futures : stories / Ryan Habermeyer.
Description: First edition. | Rochester, NY : BOA Editions, Ltd., 2018.
Identifiers: LCCN 2017044814 | ISBN 9781942683605 (pbk. : alk. paper)
Classification: LCC PS3608.A2396 A6 2018 | DDC 813/.6—dc23
LC record available at https://lccn.loc.gov/2017044814

BOA Editions, Ltd.
250 North Goodman Street, Suite 306
Rochester, NY 14607
www.boaeditions.org
A. Poulin, Jr., Founder (1938–1996)

*For Jenna, who believes in a future with unicorns.*

We are the children of chaos, and the deep structure of change is decay. At root, there is only corruption, and the unstemmable tide of chaos. Gone is purpose; all that is left is direction. This is the bleakness we have to accept as we peer deeply and dispassionately into the heart of the Universe.

—Peter Atkins, *The Second Law*

# Contents

A Cosmonaut's Guide
to Microgravitic Reproduction     9

The Foot     24

Visitation     40

Frustrations of a Coyote     49

Everything You Wanted to Know
About Astrophysics but Were Too Afraid to Ask     66

Indulgences     74

Ellie's Brood     78

What the Body Does
When It Doesn't Know What Else to Do     89

St. Abelard's Zoo for Endangered Species     98

The Good Nazi Karl Schmidt     115

A Genealogical Approach to My Father's Ass     123

Your Tragedy Is Important to Us     125

The Fertile Yellow     128

Veyo, Forgotten by the Mormons     138

An Unfinished Man     146

Valdosta, After the Flood     156

In Search of Fortunes Not Yet Lost     164

The Catapult of Tooele     177

Neophytes     192

❖

Acknowledgments     209
About the Author     213
Colophon     216

# A Cosmonaut's Guide to Microgravitic Reproduction

The job notice was simple: COSMONAUTS WANTED. NO EXPE-RIENCE NECESSARY. I was looking for gainful employment. It seemed like a good opportunity in a recession-proof industry. I've had all sorts of jobs. I've been a plumber, bike messenger, food taster, data entry clerk, window display model at a mortuary, pharmaceutical test subject, grocery bagger, and hospital janitor. I sold life insurance. For two months I was even a caretaker at a pet cemetery, but the sadness of it all nearly crushed me.

But cosmonaut! All my life I have been in love with the sky. As a boy I wore a space helmet made out of a cardboard box to the retro science fiction serials playing at the local theater. When I was nine I drafted my first design for a fully-functioning light saber and sent the blueprints to Lockheed Martin. I never heard back, but that didn't stop me from earning average grades in my high school physics class. I had never heard of the company sponsoring the cosmonaut training, but anyone willing to put a man in the sky was where I wanted to be. If not now, when?

I sold my things. I moved out of my apartment. I called the number on the flier. There was a phone interview. They sent a questionnaire. They took tissue samples. They studied my blood and male fluids. The Psych Department profile came back in the acceptable range. They purchased me a plane ticket to come to the facility at the end of the month. "Say goodbye to your loved ones," the HR woman told me. "You may be gone awhile."

The night before I left I had a date with a girl. Her name was Naomi. We shared a few acquaintances. They thought we might be a good match. She was intrigued by my new job.

"What will you do?"

"Probably science," I said, my mouth full of alfredo sauce.

Naomi seemed nervous, twirling her fork in her noodles.

"My parents are dead," I told her. "My grandmother is in a home. My brother got blown up in the war."

"Why are you telling me this?" she wanted to know. I could sense she did not go on many dates and was unfamiliar with the social custom of meaningless chitchat.

"They told me to say goodbye to my loved ones. I don't have any loved ones left." I took a deep breath and swallowed. "You're all I got."

"We just met," she blushed.

"I don't want to be launched into outer space without having someone to love down here. Love is a balloon, my father always said. It carries you away and bursts when you least expect it. I need to be tethered. That's the way my heart works."

Naomi stared at me. "I've never dated someone who," she paused, choosing her words carefully, "communicates." She chewed more noodles. She drank more wine.

When dinner was over I invited her for coffee at my loft but she said she was tired. I said the coffee could keep her up but she kissed me on the cheek and told me some other time. She must not have been much of a coffee drinker.

"Can I write you while I'm away?" I asked before she got in the taxi.

She stared at me like I was halfway between crazy and genius, like I was a little romantic but maybe a little creepy.

You know, the kind of looks Stephen Hawking writes about in his memoirs.

"Give me a sign you're up there and I'll be waiting for it," Naomi said. She kissed me again on the cheek. It has been four hundred and eighty-seven days since we were last together. I have not exactly been faithful. The problem is accountability. The problem, I am discovering after four hundred and eighty-seven days adrift in this capsule somewhere between the thermosphere and the moon, is one of basic accountability. I have no accounts of Naomi's behavior. She is ignorant of my data log despite my best efforts to relay a sign of my condition. Relationships are difficult unless you define the relationship by making accounts of who is doing what and who feels what and when and why. Yet each day I settle the accounts on my cosmological mission. We must take into account the vacuum of space. We must take into account the angular velocity in geosynchronous orbit. We must take into account the beauty of the stars. We must take into account we will arrive at day four hundred and eighty-eight and nothing will be gained nor lost and despite my best efforts and enumerations, despite all my accounting, we are one day closer to extinction.


Training lasted three days. There were eleven of us in the beginning. We had all seen the advertisement, flier 14-307-1792. We had all been extended invitations. Upon arrival we were administered a second round of medical assessments. Two candidates were disqualified. One was too tall. The other failed a vision test. That placed us all on alert. Only the best would advance.

A series of exercises followed. We treaded water in full cosmonaut suits for six hours. We were subject to extreme temperatures. We were locked in a room with small animals and told there was only enough oxygen for one of us. Decisions were made. Morals were questioned. By the end of the first day only five cadets remained.

The second day involved flight simulations and preliminary microgravity experiments. We were taken to the launching facility. From the outside it looked like a grain silo. Inside were lots of machines. Men and women in lab coats paced around the machinery with their clipboards. There was a persistent noise. It smelled like someone had spilled cola on the electrical outlets.

They introduced us to the space capsules. These were large, spherical orbs. The outer shell was made of a kind of durable plastic or experimental metal. There were three viewing windows. The orbs were attached to a rocket propulsion system. It looked like a network of wires and tubing and circuitry plugged into a series of outlets. It was remarkable.

To acquaint us with the system we watched a launch simulation performed on a monkey. We were not allowed to visit the launching site, but a video camera allowed us to see inside the simulation capsule using a simultaneous broadcast. It was a very seasoned monkey, a descendant of one of the first monkeys launched into space by the Russians. He looked very cute in his hand-tailored monkey spacesuit.

The monkey did not survive the third simulation. It started screeching and then the video transmission failed. We stared, unblinking, at the black screen. Someone said it was a malfunction. But was it the monkey or the capsule? Nobody could say. One of the cadets excused himself from consideration and left the facility. And then there were four of us.

We spent the remainder of the second day in trial launches. The first of these was the most frightening. Thankfully, I was not the first cadet. That privilege belonged to Atwater.

We watched from the control room as they strapped him into the capsule. He was shown the adjoining escape pod. He was given some brief instructions on using the controls. Then the capsule door closed. Atwater looked directly at the camera. He seemed serene, like an angel who knew his place was among the stars. He waved. We waved back.

We asked the launch director how fast Atwater would be traveling. We also wanted to know how high into the atmosphere he would reach. The launch director shrugged.

"However fast and high the propulsion system launches him."

During the launch the reception of Atwater's video transmission began to blur. Within a few minutes the screen was black. We waited a few hours to receive word about the success of the launch. The reconnaissance team returned with a few splintered pieces of wood and clumps of tinfoil. These were analyzed. We received no further transmissions from Atwater.

Now there were three of us. The directors congratulated us. We were the best of the best, a holy trinity of sorts.


Now that we are in orbit, training all seems like a dream. It is only Saratov and I in the capsule. Obermeier, the third wheel of our trinity, received the unnameable assignment elsewhere. We are shipmates, me and Saratov, anxiously engaged in the completion of our mission.

It is cramped in the capsule. The main control room is shaped like an egg and from top to bottom is roughly twelve feet. Attached to the main capsule orb is the research chamber full of cables, elastic belts and inflatable tunnels. It is also shaped like an egg but not as spacious. Saratov erroneously calls it the emergency escape pod, but Saratov is not well and easily confused. I never got a good look at the capsule from the outside before launch, but I imagine to extraterrestrial life forms we look like two sad testicles castrated and floating in the great womb of space.

Saratov is less poetic than I am. As we drift in our relentless orbit I point out the stars whose light comes through the window dull as ice cream and compare it to the light of the sun which at certain times of the day overwhelms the senses. Saratov calls me an idiot. Saratov says it is obvious the stars have been cut out of paper, the glare of the sun is just a man with a flashlight, and all that wonderful black womb of space was created by an intern with a magic marker because we are prisoners in somebody's sick experiment.

"Open your eyes," she tells me. "Stop dreaming."

I don't think Saratov is well.

Saratov is the calculator. I am the enumerator. This is our mission: to calculate and enumerate. I have always been good with numbers. This is how I distinguished myself in training. The Chief Designer singled me out. He told me having distinguished myself I would be joining an international mission with Saratov. I told him it sounded very dangerous to go into space with a Russian.

"We're cosmonauts, son," the Chief Designer said. "There are always going to be Russians in the cosmos. That's why we need to send our very best. It is a special mission."

"What makes it special?" I wanted to know.

"All that will be revealed at a later date," he said.

Then he shook my hand. The Chief Designer actually shook my hand.

And here we are. Saratov makes calculations but she is not so good with numbers. As she makes calculations, keeping us on the appropriate trajectory, she shouts out a number. I remember that number until she asks me to repeat it and insert it back into her equations. After finishing her calculations she flips a switch to deliver the transmission signal to those on earth to track our position. This is what we must do. Humanity depends on it. Saratov then relays this information through the radio. She says, "Did you receive our transmission?" Sometimes she will transmit unofficial information, her favorite being, "I don't see any god up here." Like I said, Saratov is not well.

But what can be done? These are the accounts. We all have our assignments and perhaps Saratov's is not to be well. I have faith this will all be confirmed at a later date.

Only a few days after our launch I awoke and found Saratov with a knife to my throat. She demanded to know what my assignment was. I told her I was the enumerator. She said that was a lie. I admitted it was a half-truth. I said I was also here for research purposes, like her, and pointed to the mice and geckos and fishes in their respective cages inside the research chamber. She took the knife away from my throat. Our relationship has been a bit strained since then.

My true assignment is microgravitic reproduction. This assignment was given to me by the Chief Designer. When he called me into his office he inquired about my romantic status. I told him about Naomi. He told me the mission would require being unfaithful to Naomi, but sometimes science demands a little infidelity for the sake of the truth.

He let me read Document 12-571-3570 in the handbook. It detailed all previous experiments involving microgravitic reproduction. Apparently, the company had been running experiments for decades. The Chief Designer explained our sun was dying and the survival of the human species depended on interplanetary colonization. But interplanetary colonization requires perfection of microgravitic reproduction. Without microgravitic reproduction—space sex, for the neophyte—all would be lost. As recorded in Document 12-571-3570, a computer algorithm had determined the one hundred and eleven positions most compatible for sexual intimacy in microgravitic environments. Most positions had been tested on mice and geckos and Japanese koi, but less than twenty had been performed in human trials. This was our mission. Saratov and I would continue these trials. We would test hypotheses trying to determine the appropriate calculations for successful microgravitic reproduction. Then we would return and report.

"So you want me to have sex with Saratov?"

"We want you," the Chief Designer said, "to reproduce."

Before I could express my skepticism the Chief Designer told me it would be an important contribution to science. Then he hugged me. The Chief Designer actually hugged me.

"But how will I know how to seduce Saratov?"

"All that will be revealed at a later date," the Chief Designer told me.

Microgravitic reproduction is difficult, even for a man of science like me. I have attempted to follow the guidelines in the handbook, but so far we have not been very successful.

The routine is simple. Each microgravitic copulation effort begins with the same exercises. I drink a gallon of fluid from the compartment. I perform my breathing exercise until my heart rate is a steady sixty-eight. I massage my scrotum. I consult the protocol in the handbook and memorize the instructions. Then I am ready to enter the research chamber.

The research chamber is full of cables, elastic belts, and inflatable tunnels. There is a cushioned object in the center which may be applied for comfort. Lying in the research chamber at the proper angle I can see the stars through the window. It is rather romantic.

The cosmonaut's handbook is very precise. Each entry is a single page. Each page is equal to one day's worth of reproductive activities. Each entry stresses the importance of exactness, provides a description of the position, and explains the necessary postcoital de-escalation techniques to ensure maximum success and avoid medical complications. There is always an illustration.

It has become apparent that microgravitic reproduction can only be successful if both parties are consenting. In four hundred and eighty-seven days I have successfully seduced Saratov twenty-seven times, all with the assistance of wine. In each coital-trial we required the assistance of a copulation apparatus, and each coital-trial proved ineffective. Ergo, sex in space is not as easy as it might appear.

Saratov says I am a fool. Saratov says that by all calculations microgravitic reproduction is inconceivable. She says it does not matter if consenting adults use the Dancing Judy or the Blind-Eye Harriet position. It is equally useless, Saratov tells me: the final frontier was not created for humans.

It is possible she is trying to sabotage my efforts. When I am in the research chamber alone I cannot verify Saratov's calculations. Her handwriting looks like childish squiggles. I do not know if Saratov is completing her assignment or sabotaging mine, or if she is charting directions home or setting us on a course into the sun. With Saratov, there is no telling.

Regardless of whether I am able to seduce Saratov on any given day, I am still expected to perform reproductive exercises. For those occasions when Saratov refuses intimacy, there is a simulator. It is a bulky apparatus and not very pleasant. The handbook directions are simple. I place my genitals into the reproductive port. I assume the experimental position as outlined in the cosmonaut handbook. I release my fluids. I have nothing else to say about the simulator, other than the handbook lists these activities as transatmospheric reproduction. The handbook says the fluid deposits can survive the extreme conditions of the vacuum of space. The handbook also says that transatmospheric reproduction is the fail-safe option because perhaps, if all else fails, the fluids will continue in their trajectories across the galaxy and be discovered by an advanced civilization which can resurrect our species when our sun dies.

It is easy to get discouraged on days of transatmospheric reproduction. But I trust in the Chief Designer. I trust that Saratov will see my diligence and one day wish to join me in the research chamber of her own volition so together we might multiply and replenish the earth.


Saratov might be pregnant.

Last night was the first night we successfully performed microgravitic reproduction without the assistance of wine. Perhaps I benefited from Saratov's desperation. I noticed she was more moody than usual. Saratov often cried. She had stopped making calculations and just stared out the window, looked at the stars, and cried. They were beautiful, but not worth that many tears.

Yesterday when I asked why she was crying she hugged me. Saratov actually hugged me. It was my first human touch in a long time. Then she kissed me. It felt almost alien.

We stumbled into the research chamber. We did not utilize the *Cosmonaut's Guide for Microgravitic Reproduction*. We experimented. Saratov wore a cosmonaut helmet with the visor down. A strange thing happened. It was wonderful. Saratov was very sincere. I was very adept.

Afterwards she wanted to cuddle. It was just the two of us, pulled apart by zero gravity but managing to find our way back to each other. Before I forget I must make an account of the microgravitic reproductive performance review. Be advised, I have yet to review the videotape, thus the suggestions are inconclusive and the analysis not comprehensive:

INITIATE RELATIONS WHEN HELPMATE IS CRYING. THIS CONFIRMS THE CHIEF DESIGNER'S SUGGESTION IN TRAINING TO "ENGAGE THEM WHEN THEY'RE VULNERABLE."

REST BETWEEN SESSIONS AT 4-HOUR INTERVALS. SESSIONS CONDUCTED WITHOUT AT LEAST ONE HOUR REST PERIOD WILL AFFECT HAND-EYE-COORDINATION.

SUBJECTS REPORTED IMPROVED RESULTS IN ZERO-G WHEN PROPERLY HYDRATED, PREFERABLY SOMETHING CARBONATED. FURTHER RESEARCH IS NEEDED ON CORRELATION BETWEEN CARBONATION AND LOCALIZED SUBTRANSVERSAL PLANE TISSUE SENSITIVITY. SEE APPENDIX II-C.

EMPLOYING THE HYDRAULIC THERMAL SENSORS AT REGULAR INTERVALS ASSISTS HELPMATE WITH ANORGASMIA.

DISREGARD EXERCISES #42-A AND #326-C IN HANDBOOK. HELPMATE HAS ADVISED THERE IS ONLY ONE OFFICIAL PORT OF ENTRY. ALL OTHER PORTS ARE DESIGNATED AS NON-EXPERIMENTAL. FOR FURTHER ANALYSIS, PLEASE SEE APPENDIX III.

DEGRASSE-TYSON™ DUAL ELASTIC BELTS AROUND THE WAIST ARE VERY EFFECTIVE AT OVERCOMING

SUBJECT-TO-SUBJECT SUSPENSION IN ZERO-G, BUT DIFFI-
CULT TO MAINTAIN OVER EXTENDED PERIODS OF TIME.
ELASTIC BELTS BINDING THIGH-TO-WAIST IS EFFECTIVE,
BUT AFFECTS EMOTIONAL CONDITION OF HELPMATE WHO
FEELS SHE IS IN A SNUFF FILM. CHAFFING IS, HOWEVER,
MINIMAL IN SUCH CONFIGURATIONS, WHICH IS A BONUS
(DEPENDING ON MOOD). FOR MORE DETAILED INFOR-
MATION PLEASE SEE POST-FLIGHT SUMMARY DOCUMENT
14-307-1792.

THERE IS NOT SUFFICIENT OXYGEN SUPPLY OR SUSTAIN-
ABLE AIR PRESSURE IN THE INFLATABLE TUNNEL FOR TWO
IMMEDIATE SEQUENTIAL SESSIONS. MALE SUBJECT PASSED
OUT AND HAD TO BE REVIVED.

IN THEORY, THE GYSSLINGER-VELASCO-5564 MANIPULA-
TOR APPARATUS IS FUNCTIONAL, BUT OVER THE COURSE
OF THREE DIFFERENT EXPERIMENTAL CONFIGURATIONS
SUBJECTS CONCLUDED THE APPARATUS IS AWKWARD AND
AT TIMES PAINFUL TO OPERATE. PRACTICALITY OF THE
DEVICE IS THUS QUESTIONED. ADHERING TO THE DESIGNS
OF THE MANIPULATOR DURING SESSION 3 RESULTED IN
MALE SUBJECT'S HEAD BETWEEN HELPMATE'S THIGHS
WHICH, WHILE SUCCESSFUL FOR INCREASING EMOTIONAL
ATTACHMENT BETWEEN PARTIES, IS UNPRODUCTIVE FOR
THE PURPOSES OF MICROGRAVITIC REPRODUCTION. FUR-
THER DIRECTIVES ON HOW TO OPERATE THE MANIPULA-
TOR IS REQUESTED.

FOREPLAY CONFIGURATION #218-B (I.E., LAZY SUSAN)
IS INEFFECTIVE AND UNAPPEALING FOR BOTH PARTIES.

POSTCOITAL SUSPENDED DISCHARGE IN ZERO-G IS A

PROBLEM. CLEANING APPARATUS (HAWKING XM-0012 VAC-
UUM?) MUST BE MADE AVAILABLE FOR FUTURE MISSIONS.

Saratov is missing. I must have fallen asleep. I rarely sleep.
I distinguished myself in training by not sleeping for eleven
days straight. There is no way to account for Saratov's absence.
She is not in the research chamber. She is not in her seat at
the control panel. She is not making calculations. The hatch
is closed. The evidence is incontrovertible: Saratov is missing.

I know the directives. In the appendix of *The Cosmonaut's
Guide to Microgravitic Reproduction* is a list of directives for
every imaginable scenario. We were well-conditioned in training. We cannot exist without orders.

I should send a radio transmission explaining the miscal-
culation. If that fails I should send a distress signal. If that fails
I should recalibrate the orbit and pilot the capsule to safety.

Instead, I smash the control panel. Almost immediately I
feel the capsule spinning out of orbit. There are lights flashing.
There are sirens. I hear voices. The entire capsule is shaking
and the smashed computer screen flashes a green alien code.
I can hear myself screaming. How is this possible? There is no
sound in space. I should prepare myself for a crash landing.
I should practice my breathing and start singing "When You
Wish Upon a Star" like we had been trained.

But I panic. Or maybe I am following instinct for the
first time.

I open the hatch and let in the stars.

I survive, of course. I don't remember much immediately after opening the hatch. I am floating. Everything is perfectly
still. It is difficult to breath. I can feel the empty womb of

space closing in on me and a thousand points of light probing my body.

I wake up in a hospital bed. The walls are white. It smells like ammonia. They tell me I am dehydrated and suffering from an unidentified disequilibrium of the blood. I'm attached to a respiration system. When I inquire how I survived atmospheric reentry without disintegrating I am told only the man upstairs is privy to such details. This raises my spirits and I ask the nurse if she knows the Chief Designer and if he had come to see me, but she just smiles weakly and gives me an injection.

Recovery is swift. Within a few days I receive medical clearance. Psychologically fit, honorably discharged. This is slightly disappointing. Part of me had hoped to die in space and have an elementary school named in my honor.

There is no news from mission control. They must have collected the data they needed. Or they found someone else to colonize the galaxy. Or even for cosmonauts, real or otherwise, it's all just bureaucratic bullshit.

I rent an apartment. I grow a lame beard and eat a lot of Greek yogurt.

I search the classifieds. There is a job selling balloon animals in the park. I interview. Training lasts a few hours. The creativity is a relief, but the customers leave much to be desired and there is little opportunity for advancement in the industry.

Then, unexpectedly, one day I see Saratov. She has cut her hair and walks with a limp, but it is Saratov. She is eating a pretzel in the park and comes up to the kiosk and asks me for a balloon animal.

"What would you like?" I ask, stretching one of the balloons.

"Surprise me," she says. It's obvious she doesn't recognize me.

I twist the balloons until they make a cosmonaut helmet. There is even a visor. I help fit it over her head. Saratov is impressed, as are a few of the parents and kids watching me. They clap with slightly bemused enthusiasm.

"You're really talented," she says.

She adjusts the balloon visor and stares at me. That's when I lean forward to kiss her. Maybe we could initiate a rogue experiment. Maybe with a little gravitational pull we could make this work.

# The Foot

A foot was recovered from the inlet. Nobody was sure how long it had been there. A married couple from the city who had come to see what the tide brought in had spotted a dark shape along a sandbar not far from the shore. They alerted the authorities who, because of the late September fog, dismissed the foot as the remains of the old lighthouse and saw no reason for alarm. It was not until a small group of curiosity seekers rowed out to the sandbar that they realized it was a human foot.

The next morning a group of men from the public works department with proper equipment began to excavate the foot from where it was half-trenched in the shoal. A crowd of us watched from the mainland pier like a flock of filthy birds, waiting for the next ferry to carry us across the bay. We joined a few dozen other sightseers, all of us desperate for a closer view. When the mechanical crane hauling the foot finally succeeded in wrenching it out of a small tide pool we cheered. It was loaded onto a small barge. The crane then hoisted the foot into the air where it dangled for a moment before being dragged along the beach where it was positioned between two small sand dunes on an otherwise rocky shoreline.

We let out a collective gasp.

The foot was enormous. It was at least twice as tall as the nearest water tower, and as wide as a cluster of neighborhood streets. It was covered in a crust of sea slime and severed above the ankle. The foot smelled of ash and cardamom, lacking the odor of decomposition one might expect. It was a left foot and we wanted to believe this was significant. The fourth toe was badly mangled, but whether it had been broken from our dragging it ashore or devoured by sharks was uncertain. The only other visible damage was a circular wound in the heel fouled with sea waste and discolored by sunlight. Most of the foot was wreathed in seaweed. Many onlookers found it appalling and retreated from the beach, terrified at what else might wash ashore. The rest of us held our throats, unsure if the foot had fallen out of the sky or been belched from the ocean depths.

For the first few hours nobody dared disturb the foot. Several men from the city sanitation department stood near the heel, plotting the best way to dispose of the creature. The rest of us studied it from a distance. Surprisingly, rigor mortis had not yet set and we saw, with a playful horror, how the toes occasionally twitched. We assumed this was simple biology, but the more imaginative among us suspected it was an attempt at rudimentary communication.

Terrified by this monstrosity we walked up and down the shore. We kicked up sand. Later we stood erect, hands to our eyes to shield them from the sun, trying not to blink out of fear the vision might be taken from us. The foot's beauty was equaled only by its monstrosity and we could not escape the feeling we were in the presence of a real Cinderella.

At high tide large pools of brackish water gathered around the foot, and the receding waves did their best to slowly pull the foot back out to sea. But the foot, as if sensing our curiosity, settled into the sand comfortably. As we admired the foot it seemed suddenly afflicted with a profound sense of shame. Nobody could say what horrors had led to its predicament, and such ignorance filled us with the deepest sympathy.

We exchanged speculative hypotheses. Some were fanciful and said it was from a sciapode mentioned in medieval nautical logs. Others suggested when the towers collapsed earlier this month the remains of some victims must have exploded out to sea. A historian among us was convinced it belonged to the Egyptian deity Osiris and we could expect more pieces to surface.

"When the cock washes up you come and find me," one of the women sighed.

A timid circle formed around the foot. We wandered cautiously around it with a mixture of arousal and repulsion. There was a childish hope that so much walking might lure the foot into motion. We were at a loss for words. There were no antecedents for this sort of thing. Had it been an alien spacecraft we would have known the proper models of behavior. We would have panicked—set fire to buildings and thrown babies from the rooftops. We would have prayed for deliverance. We would have alerted the military to recover supplies of Agent Orange. Eventually, we would have submitted to our overlords of little green men. But this was a foot. We were quiet. We were confused. There were no protocols. This was no invasion—it was an unexpected alien visitation.

The foot had an infectious presence. More and more visitors arrived in their Sunday best.

As we approached the heel which was turned seaward we could not help but feel uneasy with the foot's sheer size. Our own feet were sad facsimiles of this unidentified leviathan, and we marveled at how much distance such a foot might cover in a single step. We had long prided ourselves on the reach of our gaze, but not until now had we looked at our own footprints in the sand as those of travelers shackled to an inescapable gravity.

Nobody had been close enough to touch the foot when there was a murmur from the crowd. Someone shouted and soon all were pointing in the direction of the foot. We were surprised to see a child waving at us from one of the pinkie toes. He was an almost unnoticeable spot. Other children soon appeared. We called to them, but they ignored us, whispering among themselves. They pelted us with rocks.

A few hours later the children reappeared, this time on the tip of the hallux, and through a series of shouts and gestures we convinced them to climb down the web of seaweed clinging to the skin. We tried to persuade them to talk but they first pretended to be confused, then refused to cooperate. They claimed to be stowaways from a distant planet and accused us of trying to abduct them. Only after prying through their imaginative wall did they confess to having discovered the foot yesterday while rowing in the inlet. One of the girls had wandered inside the foot through a flap of skin and the rest of them, mistaking it for a crashed flying saucer, had alternated between playing games of hide-and-seek and trying to locate the navigational system in an effort to fly the spacecraft back to their home planet. The children expressed disappointment when we assured them they were all too human and still on this lousy planet Earth, but were obviously delighted to be escorted away by authorities dressed in biohazard outfits.


We arrived early the following morning. There had been some worry about what might happen to the foot during the night. Despite the makeshift rigging to secure the foot in place, there were no guarantees.

We were relieved to find the foot as we had left it. It stood motionless with the weary look of an insomniac. Our hesitation was soon replaced by an enthused curiosity. We continued to circle the foot cautiously, afraid at intimate contact but eager to plumb the depths of this tragedy. More and more people rushed forward, touched the foot, then hurried back to the crowd. This went on for most of the morning. There were cautions against such recklessness and a few of the older visitors chided the younger tourists, insisting that at any moment the foot might take a step and crush them. The teenagers ignored such warnings and indulged in their fascination, too young to be concerned by how the world makes Frankensteins of us all.

The tide changed and water pooled around the foot. Often the heel would sink into the wet sand, giving the impression the foot was moving of its own volition in half turns, but by low tide the sand had dried and the foot rested steadily in place. When it tilted to one side or the other we took advantage to study the arch which frustrated us with its vast anatomy.

By mid-afternoon the foot was littered with spectators. Many of these enthusiasts shouted at friends from their perch on the toes, while the more adventurous wandered inside the toenail that was mildly rancid with the first hint of decomposition. Occasionally, the muscles in the foot would spasm and the tremors sent people falling off the foot this way and that. A few were hospitalized with minor injuries. Most brushed the sand from their clothes and laughed before climbing back onto the foot.

The indisputable existence of the foot induced irrational fears that our own limbs might abandon us, but we comforted ourselves with the knowledge that it takes a lot of effort to make a body disappear, and even when it's gone you feel it two steps beside you.

A handful of us decided to explore the uncharted regions of the foot. We started along the pinkie toe and made our way across the epidermal webbing before turning east and attempting to scale the instep. As we climbed we noticed several children had converted the instep into a slide. Climbing higher the seaweed was brittle and pulled away with ease. We huddled close to the skin and took note of the helix of blood vessels beneath the surface. One of the men in our company used a knife to open a fold of skin and gently slipped his hand inside.

"It's still warm," he smiled.

Walking along the foot was deeply satisfying. We walked with a new understanding of gravity, now more than ever before aware of the pettiness of our own feet. Near the peak where the foot had been severed from the leg the skin folded back and the bone became visible. We saw where the foot was knit together by tendon and ligament. It was the first time any of us had given any thought that our own bodies were an inexplicable maze that would never be solved. From our vantage point near the summit we could see a few hundred yards across the bay to the city. The buildings looked like strange appendages surging out of the ground.

We made it back down the foot and to the beach just before nightfall, just in to time to discover a heated debate among the crowds. Everybody had a theory about the foot. Some insisted it was an error of nature. The more religious warned us that when the devil is on the loose he goes barefoot. For the pathologists who had been commissioned by the city the foot was in irresistible specimen. They established a quarantine perimeter and circled the foot for hours making notes in their spreadsheets. We could not tell if they were performing an analysis or waiting to be acknowledged by the foot. They extracted samples for traces of typhoid and cholera, but the foot lacked any conclusive epidemiology.

"Disease is a strange magic," they told us. "It is the one thing that will never disappear."

Many of the pathologists had spent their careers in quarantine facilities where they had seen immigrants with feet ruined by various journeys. They related how the immigrants spoke dozens of languages but their feet, blistered and swollen and bleeding and twisted, told a similar story of pain and loss. Those with gangrene were sent to the surgical wing there they discovered amputation was the worst magic trick of all. The pathologists produced photographs from the municipal archives of crates full of severed feet destined for the furnaces.

The foot displayed no indication it was a migrant, but neither was it a native of anything imaginable. We wondered if the foot had at one time belonged to one of the migrants who once lived in a quarantine facility. Perhaps it had been amputated and accidentally pitched into the inlet instead of the furnace and over the years grew with rage and love until it finally returned, looking for the body it had lost. We wanted to believe this theory most of all.

Within a few days access to the foot became more difficult. Visitors required permits and tour guides monopolized the regulated public viewing sessions. Tickets were expensive. Children were frequent loiterers around the foot and orchestrated elaborate attempts to breach security. Many seemed hopeful it was not a foot but the flying saucer they had been waiting for. For as much as we admired their tenacity we could not bring ourselves to disrespect the foot with such frivolity.

More crowds appeared and they became more peculiar. Authorities removed a group of teenagers for stomping on the cuticle of the big toe in what was deemed a coordinated attack of attempted larceny. An elderly couple shuffled around the heel, pausing to compare their wrinkles with the wrinkles on the foot. And newlyweds necked on the blister between the third and fourth toes. Several young boys, removed from playing on the foot, perched on the dunes a short distance away and watched the crowds. They twisted their bare feet into the sand and shook their heads in frustration.

The first of many weepers arrived. These people stood a good distance from the foot and wept in its presence. They came to feel like victims. They had no genuine interaction with the foot beyond a simple touch. They never climbed the foot to its summit where the bone was exposed and looked down into the cavity that was deep, like a wishing well, and were horrified by the abyss of their own bodies. They wished for the foot to smother them in sorrow.

Through all these visitations the foot maintained its silent composure.

Just before sunset on the fourth day a woman pointed to the sky at the first sight of the egrets.

"Here they come," she said.


With the arrival of the birds it became necessary to organize a task force of volunteers to clean the foot and preserve it from contamination. Scaffolding was erected and spotlights positioned so the labor could continue around the clock. They called us scabs. That is what we looked like to the spectators below—tiny, migratory scabs. It was a Herculean task.

We began by removing the seaweed and unidentified sea waste. Beneath this layer we discovered a crust of barnacles. Armed with chisels, we proceeded carefully. The scientists worried the scrubbing might compromise the foot's integrity and accelerate decomposition. In the callused areas the barnacles had become stubborn. It was a delicate process: scrape too forcefully and the skin tore, too gently and the blade snapped. Some skinning was unavoidable. It was not uncommon for the flesh to gently yield and pockets of foul gas burst like miniature geysers. After scraping away the barnacles and other crusts, we washed the area with rags soaked in a mixture of Epsom salts and lemon oil until the skin appeared sickly white. There was nothing fetishistic about this. We took measurements and tissue samples. We made notes for the report and delivered these to the scientists. Then we proceeded to the next area.

Initial calculations were conflicting. Whereas before the pathologists had been confident the foot must succumb to the principles of cellular degeneration, the foot now resisted such easy biology. At a cellular level the foot appeared to be still alive: absorbing, reproducing, struggling to adapt to its new reality. Nobody knew if the rate of growth would outpace the rate of decomposition. It might turn to dust or it could fill the world.

We maintained the conviction that there was some form beneath the tangles of seaweed worth discovering. Our lives that had been so anonymous were suddenly qualitative and not merely quantitative. We could define ourselves in relation to the foot—as devoted servants our lives were subsidiaries of its absoluteness. We scraped barnacles and scrubbed the skin believing there was some connection between us and the foot. Did we not share a comparable anatomy? It was a tragedy just beyond our grasp, all the more attractive because at any moment we felt the foot's fate might be our own. Its predicament did not seem the result of some evolutionary process, but a sociological error for which we must be the perpetrators.

There were many other hypotheses as well as records of what the foot did and did not do, which if we had written them down in the reports would fill a library.

By the end of the month we had finished our initial cleaning. There was no celebration. Almost immediately we made plans for a second cleaning as we realized the skin became coarse from sea breeze, a dull yellow the color of headaches. If we wished to preserve the foot it would require constant moisturizing. Nobody was upset. Like cheerful stone masons constructing the great pyramids, we felt part of a sublime and endless labor.

The skeptics said it was a pointless exercise. They ridiculed us. What had we discovered? The foot had eleven calluses, four bruises, six blisters, three dimples, and forty-seven scratches. But it remained a foot—a fat, grotesque, ungodly foot. We were nothing more than God's pedicurists—six days a week in fourteen-hour shifts. For what? Even we were not quite sure, we only knew we must.

The foot continued to elude our understanding. Definitive conclusions into its character were disappointingly slim. It was a woman's foot. Most likely late middle age. A small burn scar near the heel led us to believe she had at one time been a smoker. Other vices were indeterminate. The faint residue of orange nail polish indicated she was an impulsive woman, while her third phalange was both bent and longer than the hallux, the hallmark of a creative but troubled mind. All the toes were angled in the Egyptian style. She had properly cared for her toes and we found no sign of ingrowth in the nails. Perhaps it was the way the spotlights illuminated new regions of the foot, or just our familiarity with its presence, but we detected a subtle change in the foot's demeanor. Stripped of the barnacles and seaweed the foot seemed naked. From this moment there was something vain about the foot, a kind of unapologetic decadence.

The exact nature of the foot's demise remained elusive. We ruled out suicide. Natural causes seemed unlikely. With an asphyxiation the toes would have curled with greater intensity. If she had drowned the superficial epidermis would have been saturated. There was no indication of an infection or surgical amputation. We made no sense of the pattern of epidermal folds where the foot had been severed other than the possibility the injury was produced by an explosion.

Our inquiries were slow and meticulous. The foot demanded speculations. It demanded interpretations. It had to belong to someone. It had to be missed. It could not just be a foot. Could it?

Thankfully, we discovered a distinguishing feature: a freckle in the shape of a half-moon just above the ankle. It was a crucial detail as, suddenly, we remembered a girl with a similar freckle.

Her name was Ada. She had grown up in the orphanage. This was many years ago. She had a contagious smile. Before the orphanage she had been in recovery at the quarantine facility. Before quarantine she had sailed across the Atlantic with her brother as a stowaway. Both her parents had been blown up in the war. After looking at the plantar aspect on her brother's right foot the last night on the ship, she warned him not to be the first one to see the coastline. Fearful of his sister's foresight, the boy hid in the boiler room and accidentally slipped and got blown out of the steam stacks in a thousand pieces. Ada lived with the certainty that one day she would also be blown up.

"I can feel it in my feet," she said. "You can't escape genealogy."

Ada dreamed of being famous, like the German actresses in old silent films. She wanted to perform in concert halls and opera houses. She wanted her name on billboards in faraway places.

The orphanage was a different kind of quarantine and Ada had the most infectious disease of all: she walked. She walked to the cafeteria for her meals. She walked to the small chapel where on Tuesdays the chaplain set up a movie projector. She walked out of her bed in the morning and into it at night. She walked on the bed. She was often found sleepwalking. It didn't matter if she was walking down a hallway or shuffling circles in her room, there was something about the way Ada walked. She never seemed to be in a hurry or lost. She walked through doors and down hallways singing songs in a raggedy dress she refused to change because she liked the smell of boiler room smoke and ash. It was as if she had transcended the need for feet yet used them in a way never before imagined.

At night she told stories to her quarantined neighbors of the places her feet had taken her. Everyone listened spellbound. Rumors started she had walked across the Atlantic. She let many of the orphans admire her feet. They touched her toes, or kissed the freckle on her ankle, or brushed the instep clean with their hair. They wanted her to look at their own feet. She told the orphans their fortunes like a trained podomancist. No chocolate on Tuesdays for you, she said to one. Never get on a bicycle in Boston, she said to another. Find love with a red-headed baker wearing a size nine but not the stockbroker with a size twelve, she told someone. Occasionally, a false promise slipped in here and there but this was to be expected.

"It's a shame we were not born as yaks," Ada said. "Hooves are more clairvoyant than toes."

We were still cleaning the foot, daydreaming of Ada, when the lab reports returned and the freckle proved to be nothing more than a minor skin irritation that flaked away after weeks in the sun.

The newspaper rescinded its obituary of the orphan girl and the talk radio programs revived wild speculations about the foot's potential identity. A sentimental, made-for-television miniseries about the foot aired to popular acclaim. There were very few conversations in town that did not devolve into debates about the foot.

Now that the foot once more lacked an identity people seemed anxious. When we believed it was Ada we had felt ourselves moving towards relief, towards closure. We were ready to return to our normal lives, to lives with just our own two feet and the ground beneath them, to lives without the threat of more appendages, more extensions of ourselves surfacing. We had felt as if very soon we would have our proper ending and the foot would either be reunited with its body or we would finally penetrate the mystery of its presence. We could nod our heads. We could breathe easy knowing it was just a foot and not something of the hereafter, not something tragic, not something else entirely. We looked forward to forgetting. Now all that was in doubt. Now we were forced to not just acknowledge the foot, but burdened with remembering the foot and remembering into the future of its past and its relentless lives which were passing or yet to come.

For months we waited anxiously for the foot to perform some genuine Cinderella transformation but our hopes ended in disappointment. We came no closer to penetrating its mystery. Any data collected merely pointed to a new set of variables and a bifurcation of hypotheses. The foot maintained a habitual silence, oblivious to our tired amazement.

And so the foot's intransience exhausted our mental energies. We had other fantasies at one time, but now they were all eclipsed by this tower of flesh and bone. We began to see the foot everywhere. A child at the park limped behind the others with a swollen foot. At the hospital a woman miscarried a fetus whose only distinct anatomical feature was feet. There was a new car designed in the shape of a foot, and downtown a foundation pit for new buildings looked like enormous, geometrical footprints. At one time we might have felt refreshed by such permutations, but now any reminder of the foot only served to mock our inadequacies. The foot ached with anticipation, alive in a way we were not.

Our constant attention to the foot's hygiene began to feel tedious. After months of hygienic ritual, we gave up. We had only succeeded in washing away a façade of beauty. Tours were canceled. Financing for a documentary feature on the foot fell through. Even the scientists, whose fascination was seemingly endless, lamented the foot was a mere appendage and not something more worthwhile. Most would have preferred an enormous vagina.

The crowds grew smaller and smaller. Visitors acted impatiently. A flap of skin was removed in the shape of the masonic compass. Part of a toenail was drilled away and rumors later surfaced it had been ground up and sold as an aphrodisiac in gated communities. Few were surprised when we discovered three harpoons lodged in the heel, no doubt the work of some professorial imagination who suspected it was the foot of Achilles.

Within a few months only the children were regular visitors. They climbed up and down and in and out of the decomposing leviathan with unbridled enthusiasm.

We asked ourselves whether we should have done things different. Should we have allowed it to decompose with dignity instead of this unnatural preservation that now faded to ruin? Should we have ignored it entirely and not burdened the foot with such metaphysical significance? Should we have been more respectful and wondered what the foot wanted instead of peddling our own desires? In a certain way, the foot's unconscious existence was its greatest insult of all. It existed and did not exist simultaneously, haunting us in a way that could not be stopped.

When we stepped off the ferry one evening we discovered the receding seawaters slowly dragging the foot back into the inlet. A small crowd watched in disbelief. The water pooled under the foot and softened the sand which caused the foot to twist in half-turns. With each receding wave the foot inched into deeper water. Scientists hurried to collect tissue samples left behind on the shore. Many studied the footprint before the receding waters washed it from memory. We made no effort to summon the cranes to retrieve it.

The foot drifted across the bay. For a moment it appeared as if it might sink, hidden beneath a large wave, but then it bobbed back to the surface, drifting slowly out to sea.

For a moment we despaired. We thought of the porches we had constructed on our homes where we hoped the foot would step. We thought of the new mattresses we had stuffed to allow our own feet to dangle off the edges. We thought of the wider streets that had been built to accommodate the foot's girth. We thought of all the ways the foot might have crushed the old ways of seeing and worried we were creatures incapable of being imprinted.

It was not sadness. It was resentment—resentment that the foot would treat us so poorly as to tease us with its tragedy at a distance.

A murmur groaned from the crowd. Dark shapes spotted on the foot. It was the children. They waved to us. Several could be seen leaping off the foot as it bobbed in the waves on its way out to sea. A few children somersaulted and performed other acrobatics into the water, while others regretfully abandoned their mothership. Many refused to forsake their imaginations and, perched on the toes, pointed a navigational course out to sea as if they were commanding a submarine. The children swimming ashore stumbled past us as if they were newborn aliens.

"What is it?" a woman asked.

"Just a foot," somebody said.

We gazed until the shape of the foot was lost in the glare of the fading sun, gazing until I was the only one left on the beach, unable to admit it was only a foot.

# Visitation

Naomi is not well. Her womb is on the floor, a purple throb huddled inside yesterday's newspaper. It is still steaming. This surprises me. Something that small and unused for so many years ought to be flat and icy. When it pulses the veins across its skin shudder and twitch, and each throb is like a hurried breath.

"A wandering womb," Naomi whispers.

It must have fallen out sometime during the night. I'm suddenly jealous. Part of me wishes I had a womb of my own to lose.

Naomi goes into the bathroom. I hear grunting. Then retching. The toilet flushes. She doesn't think I'm watching as she stands at the mirror and looks at her stomach. Without a womb the skin sags from her belly. She presses fingers against it, trying to feel her insides. She looks at me with this helpless face, as if to say everything is normal, only we both know it is not.

"Maybe it wandered in from the rain," Naomi says. She goes to the window, tapping a finger against her front teeth.

We pull back the curtains and let in the sun. The womb scurries across the floor. It takes an hour to catch it. We wrap the womb in a towel and put it on the table. It is wet and leaky so we place it on a salad plate. I keep a fork at the ready. Just in case.

"It's definitely yours," I say.

"How can you tell?"

"It breathes like you. Can't you tell? It's asthmatic."

We listen to the tufts of steam slip out the womb's opening.

"What should we do?" Naomi wonders.

Our rental contract says nothing about fallen wombs. The library has no self-help books. We discuss what our instincts tell us to do, but Naomi's body rejected her womb so maybe our instincts are all out of whack.

"We can't get rid of it," Naomi says. "My mother had a hysterectomy at my age, but I'm not ready." She keeps rubbing her stomach until the skin is red.

"Maybe we should eat it," I tell Naomi, half-joking. I slide the fork down to the other end of the table. "They do that in some primitive cultures you know."

"That's the placenta, you idiot."

Naomi doesn't seem to be taking this very well. It's understandable. She's lost a womb. That has to be difficult. I can't pretend like I know how to empathize. It's not like my vas deferens has ever slipped out like a stray noodle. Still, we need to keep our wits about us. We need to keep a sense of humor. This is not the time to panic.

"I never thought the body could be so cruel," she says.

"What do you mean?"

"It's like the rest of my body knew I wasn't using my womb and *bam!* it just chased it out for being a freeloader."

We entertain other possibilities: we could donate it to a community college biology lab. Take it to a homeless shelter. Offer it as a house-warming gift. Boil it on the stovetop and use the fluids as a biofuel. None of these strike us as reasonable.

We decide to keep it, despite my reluctance.

We tell nobody. The neighbors knock on the door, but we peer from behind the curtains and give dismissive gestures with our hands. There are rumors that Naomi is deathly ill, that the man visiting her this time around—me—is keeping her a prisoner. The neighbors bring casseroles and fruit baskets. Who can blame them? We're all voyeurs hoping to catch a glimpse of the misery of others.

Naomi worries this is a ruse, that in a few days they will come with pitchforks and torches and burn both her and the womb on a makeshift pyre. Secretly, I think she was expecting nursery gifts.

It is a difficult time of year to be losing wombs. There is a heat wave. It rains some, then the sun comes out and we're smothered in humidity. We live in one of those old Victorian houses built well before the miracle of air conditioning. We open all the windows, but it's useless. Without her womb Naomi experiences an increase in body heat. She sweats all the time, her body tricked into thinking it's menopausal. The first night after we discovered the womb it slithered into the bedroom where Naomi was doing sit-ups on the floor. Me and the womb watched.

"I'll be damned if I let that thing ruin my body," she said.

I swaddled the womb inside a towel and held it close.

I suppose it's not unexpected for things to slip away. Naomi lost her wedding ring. Just slipped right off her finger. Her husband did the same, slipping out the door when Naomi least expected it. I asked her why, after all these years, she still wore the ring and she shrugged and said some habits are difficult to break. That's how we found the womb, searching for the ring under the furniture.

We lie on the floor fanning ourselves. We listen to the radio. We watch the womb. The man on the radio informs us this season has the highest rate of pregnancies.

"Asshole," Naomi says, slightly off balance as she leaves through the doorway.

I watch the womb. It feels like the womb is watching me too.

Naomi doesn't want to visit a specialist. She doesn't want to leave the house. What if there are other desertions? Her tits have been sagging for years. One of her molars is loose. I'm due for a prostate exam. We have weak hearts, decentered all too often.

"No," she says. "When a womb falls out there are consequences. It's best to ride this out on our own."

Naomi does not sleep. She sits on the sofa all night with a butterfly net and a fork. She is on one side of the room and I am on the other. This is the problem with Naomi and me. Her problems are always foreign. Most couples fight about whose turn it is to do the dishes, or which church they should attend. With Naomi it has never been that easy. What's the problem, babe? My womb. It fell out. Classic Naomi.

"Do you think I'm being punished?" she asks after we've been with the womb two weeks.

I'm quiet, unsure how to answer.

"What have you done to deserve this?" I ask.

She lists a few of her sins: she used to read pornographic romance novels to comatose widows at the nursing home. As a substitute teacher she confiscated the necklaces from all the girls in the German club and wore them every night hoping to dream their dreams. Her husband wanted a baby and she refused. When she worked at the suicide hotline she deliberately did not answer the phone. She is convinced that everybody's time comes—sooner or later, the sins add up and, in a heartbeat, something terrible and inexplicable just happens.

Early in the morning we awake to the sound of the womb bleating. We take turns massaging its misshapen edges. Sometimes I press too hard and can feel the knotted middle. It makes me hungry. The bleats get more agonizing. It keeps us awake all night. Naomi tries to feed it: used tampons, condoms, anti-birthing ointments sucked from her fingertips. Nothing satisfies it. After a few days the womb looks engorged, the frayed hairs twitching. It expels little coughs and spews pink gruel on the floor. The bleats continue, like church bells. We can't seem to figure out what the womb wants.

"What if it wants to be pregnant?" Naomi says.

We've had this conversation before. We agreed not to have children. With children, there is no guaranteed investment return on the future. You might give birth to a cardiologist, a Don Juan who likes to break hearts, or a lunatic who prefers to eat them. It's a roll of the dice. We agreed not to do that. We can't tempt nature.

I'm very firm with Naomi. "I'm not the man you're looking for."

"Men are useless," she says.

When Naomi is asleep I unknot the twists and folds of the womb. I lay them on the floor and watch them try to find each other. They're like caterpillars. They stink of little boy feet. We tried cleaning the womb in the sink but this only made the stench worse. When I've kneaded it back together it limps and flops around. It's terrified of the sunlight. I tried to take it outside for some exercise, let it roll around in the grass, but it suctioned itself to the floor and bleated like it was going to the slaughterhouse. I use a cigarette to singe the womb's underbelly and there is a high-pitch squeal, almost like something real.

I tell Naomi, "We should kill it, before it gets too aware of itself."

Naomi says we're not medically trained for that sort of thing. "Besides, we don't have a permit for its disposal."

"Just don't get too attached to it," I say.

I remind her we have to be careful about how we handle this. We could not in good conscience give the womb false hope. It's not like we planned on adopting it and enrolling it in preschool.

I'm the only one to notice the balance between them has shifted. When I first met Naomi she was a quiet woman with curves in all the right places. She was shy, but when she wanted to she could startle sunlight with her laughter. Lately, she has been thinning. I noticed it while she undressed the other night. Her bellybutton was larger than I remembered, and the skin around it had sunk into itself like a doughnut hole. The womb, however, is fatter, slightly engorged—it takes both hands to carry it. One morning, after she had swaddled the womb, I could tell the balance between them was different. Before it was like holding a papaya or mango. Now, and this is what does not make sense, when Naomi holds the womb it not only makes her appear smaller, but it is as if the womb is holding her.

She even walks around the house with an awkward tilt. She holds her breath for minutes at a time but does not pass out. She bumps into furniture. The emptiness of living without a womb is taking its toll on her, but she pretends as if nothing is wrong.

One afternoon, Naomi squats over the womb. It howls as she gets close. It doesn't want to go back. She tries to jump on it, but it scuttles away. She screams, she cries, she begs. The womb stares back at her, slightly befuddled.

Naomi reads in books that wombs respond favorably to Near Eastern spice-blends, so she eats Indian food all day but the womb is still frightened of her. When she does get her hands on it she tries insertion techniques taught to her by the adult video store clerk—the free-standing Murphy, the Russian Eagle Eye—but the womb slips out of her fingers. It's no use, I try to tell her: the womb knows better. It's not going to be another thing inside a thing.

We find a jellied discharge on the windowsill. I look at the womb. Naomi thinks it is suicidal, but I know it is trying to escape. She comes home the next day with a crib. She comes home with boards and nails and a hammer. The windows are sealed, the cupboards are fastened shut. Everything is baby-proofed. But the womb is clever. It finds a way out of the crib and falls down the stairs. It bleats and bleats.

I tell Naomi maybe it's time to take a trip to the hospital. Maybe we need a second opinion. She refuses. She says they'll slice up the womb and study it in a petri dish and she will be strapped into stirrups and probed to see if she is the next phase in human evolution.

"Is that what you want? Do you want to turn me into an alien? Do you want me to turn into Darwin's final proof?"

I hold Naomi. She cries. The womb bleats. We sit there in the hallway, the three of us holding each other. I don't know what I want. All I know is I don't have the instinct for this sort of living.

But Naomi won't deny her instincts. She is determined to be a mother. She doesn't understand the womb has outgrown us. It knows better than we do. The balance can't be restored. Despite all our reasoning, despite all our trappings, the womb escapes more and more. It scurries along the floor with tremendous speed. Other times it leaps. I use the broom to swat it away from the windows.

Then Naomi forgets to close the front door and the womb gets three blocks down the road, almost to the edge of the wood. We wrestle the womb onto the neighbor's lawn. The children on bicycles see us and scream for their mothers. A gardener tries to help, but when he sees the womb he is caught between fascination and repulsion. His hands move for his hedge clippers. We run.

Naomi complains of feeling light. She is always hungry. At meals she licks her plate clean and finishes my leftovers. Then she searches the cupboards. She eats and eats, trying to fill the void left by the womb. Now that it's clear the womb is not going back, Naomi worries she might float away. I tell her she's paranoid, but she says she's read Hippocrates and Aretaeus.

"The womb is altogether erratic," she quotes from the library book. "It knows only the logic of the animal."

"You're not an animal," I say.

"Look at me," Naomi says. "I haven't gone farther than the end of the street in a month. I'm nesting. How long until I float away?"

In bed Naomi is mean. I used to like that: a little grit, a little meanness. This is something different. She doesn't want to kiss and rejects all my attempts at foreplay. *This* is all I want, she says. Just dick.

I give her what she wants because I thought I could help her. I thought maybe if we did it enough my dick would fall off and that would make us whole—two Humpty Dumpties trying to fill the void of all our broken pieces.

I was gentle. I worried about hurting her. Soon I'm not enough. She brings home strange men. Fat men. They lock the door. I never see the same man go in there twice. I try to make her meals and bring her flowers—anything to satisfy her urges. Nothing works. Just dick.

The womb dries out. We do our best, but we're not parents. There are no more pools of fluid blotching the hardwood. The womb lies around all day pulsing in languid rhythms. Naomi pulls off brittle crusts of womb-skin and rubs them between her fingers into flakes. She massages the womb with Vaseline until it glistens. She cradles it. She sings it lullabies. No matter how much she tries to keep it moist the womb dries out.

What Naomi doesn't understand is that the womb doesn't want to be held. It wants to grow something. It wants to bring life.

One morning, while Naomi sleeps, I squeeze inside the womb. It is difficult at first, but as I'm swallowed I can see the womb regain its color and its skin turn from scaly to moist. Once inside, curled in a fetal position, I take my needle and thread and stitch the womb closed.

It's dark and warm. There is a relaxing absence of space. I tell myself it's better this way. Naomi deserves better. We need to change. We need to be different people to make this work. It's not enough to cohabit. Marriage is not enough. It's not enough for one of us to be made from the rib of another. We need to know each other inside and out. We need someone to spoil our dark, secret places. I'll wait here until the time is right. And when she least expects it, I'll crawl out into Naomi's arms, into the anonymous glow of Wednesday, and we can start over.

# Frustrations of a Coyote

Chef dragged the corpse through mud and weed and the dogs followed. Ahead was the town with its mess of gray slanted houses and shit roads and fat women on balconies, but each step in that direction felt like swimming farther and farther away, deeper and deeper into some dark pool of *idiota*. Chef limped slowly under the rot of sunless sky, ignoring the pain eating the insides of his leg. It felt warm. It felt raw. He wedged two fingers deep inside the cast and itched until the burn danced like fireworks up and down his body. He itched more. He pulled a stick off the ground, shoved it down the cast and jerked it furiously until his eyes were swimming and his head felt like jelly. He almost puked. When he heard the howls he dropped onto his stomach in the mud next to the dead man. Behind him and down the slope he could see the dark shapes trotting in the sand. They were going in circles trying to catch the scent. Chef's hands fumbled inside his pockets searching for a cigarette. He offered one to the corpse. "Hey friend, you want?" *Nada*. The dead man's face was covered with sand and a clump of seaweed hung from the neck. The dead man was quiet. It was like he was really dead.

When the dogs disappeared down the other end of the beach, Chef sat on the dead man's stomach and enjoyed his cigarette. A few tourists climbing a sand dune spotted him and waved. Chef did not wave back. When they came closer one of the tourists, a bald man dressed like a banker on holiday, asked Chef if he was having difficulties. Fucking hell, Chef laughed. What a bunch of *idiota*.

"Your friend there looks sick," the bald man said.

"We all got problems," Chef said. He jammed his fingers into the dead man's mouth and pulled them apart to force a smile.

"Jesus, that man's dead," the bald man said.

"He's no Jesus," Chef said. "This *nada* can't walk on water. He drowned. I pulled him out of the water," Chef said, nodding at the beach. "I saved him. He's mine. Now fuck off."

"Jesus, he's dead," the bald man said again. Chef laughed. The bald man and his lady friend hurried away.

Around the bend the dogs howled. Shit. They had found the scent. Chef wobbled to his feet. The wind almost knocked him over but he managed to find his balance. Chef and the drowned man kept moving, kept a steady pace ahead of the dogs that followed, kept waiting for a miserable end to this dance and wondered how in God he had ever arrived at such *idiota*.


Middle-aged and pretty much worn to guts, Chef had recently decided it was time to do something with his life. He had joined the army ten years ago hoping to find himself but instead found a scorching case of VD. When his tour finished he shot pool, drank whiskey, jerked off, cursed the government, and painted the occasional picture. He had man boobs. He lost the triple parlay by inches. His ex-girlfriend had stolen his car and was halfway to Vegas, leaving him with an assortment of Silver Surfer comics and a few Jethro Tull albums. He crashed a friend's car into a lamppost. He was in a hospital where the only channel was Telemundo and all the doctors had faces like bleeding clowns. And then he flunked the biology exam at the community college because he couldn't properly explain the differences in symbiosis between aquatic and terrestrial species? No. Hell no. The universe had pushed one button too many. Something had to be done.

He got shitfaced at the bar. Announcing his presence to his fellow bar patrons, he threatened to abuse the woman sitting next to him with his tongue, followed by a second threat to drink up the ocean and flood this establishment in his piss. Nobody listened. Chef finished his drink, saluted the barflies one last time, and declared he would walk out of this *idiota* into the deep blue sea. Good luck, the bartender said.

Swimming past the buoy, Chef discovered he was no good at drowning. He waited for a shark. He waited for the tide to suck him under. He saw a sea lion and held out his broken leg and screamed *Bite me, fucker!* but the sea lion disappeared behind a wave. He must have had some strange affinity for water because he floated miserably for more than an hour.

And then he found the corpse. It was just floating there, a fellow traveler. That was when Chef decided this was his moment of redemption: Chef the hero. Chef the savior. His ex-girlfriend had burnt all the photographs of them together saying there was nothing worth saving. She said her mother had warned her he would someday be a lousy father. He would show her. He would nurture this drowned man as if it were his own flesh and blood. By God, she would know that in suffering there was always something worth saving.

Chef and the drowned man washed ashore like mangled seaweed. Chef tried to breathe life into the man but without luck. The drowned man's face was handsome but ugly, bloated and messy like an old hamburger bun. Patches around the forehead were blistered from the sun. Two fingers had been nibbled off. The man's lips were purple, the eyes about to burst from their sockets. There was a note stuffed in the drowned man's mouth. *Our apologies to our dear friend, Fiske. A man of good taste, gone too far. Hanged, shot, stabbed, reluctantly drowned. Our apologies.*

It was only a few minutes after washing ashore that Chef heard the dogs.

Chef determined not to let this opportunity go to waste. He would not leave the drowned man on some godforsaken beach to be devoured by dogs. He had no specific plan of what to do, but Chef was confident the genius of fatherhood did not descend all at once. It may take a while to figure out the next course of action, but he had all the time in the world. For now it was simple preservation. Alone they were nobodies, but together they would be somebody.

Chef listened for a heartbeat. The drowned man had been whispering. He was sure of it. Chef never heard things. He wasn't religious. He pressed an ear close to the lips. He waited. *Nada.* "Speak up," he told the drowned man. Nope, the man was drowned.

He kept dragging the body, sometimes wondering if they were walking in circles, other times unsure if he was dragging the drowned man or if the drowned man was dragging him.

The dogs were a blur in the endless ribbons of sand. Howls came in waves, louder at first, then echoes. Chef wasn't sure where they came from. Maybe they were fascist dogs that did not approve of heroes or women in high heels. He turned in the direction of the howls, cupped his cock, and gave the mile-high salute.

Chef tore the shirt off his back. He rung out the sweat. He tied the shirt around the drowned man's wrist into a knot. This made it easier to drag him. They moved in zigzag patterns through the dunes and weeds, hoping to confuse the dogs. "My apologies, Fiske," Chef whispered.

When it was dark they hid in a ditch just below an overgrowth of wild grass. Chef gathered some rocks. When he heard howling he stumbled to his feet and hurled rocks until exhausted.

Chef and the drowned man played dead in the ditch. "Try not to look suspicious," he whispered.

He tried to dream. It was useless. His leg was on fire. And the Gestapo canines kept howling. What could they possibly want? Maybe they were coming for him. No, they wanted the drowned man. Maybe they weren't even dogs.

He patted the drowned man on the hand. "Don't let them scare you," he said. "We're gonna make it, *idiota*. You and me." The drowned man said nothing. Chef envied the drowned man's ability to dream.

There was an old phone booth about a hundred yards from the ditch. Chef stuffed the two of them inside. He was having trouble seeing. His leg throbbed. He puked all over the drowned man. He dialed numbers at random and others from memory. The voice on the other end of the phone sounded like a queer robot. It seemed unconcerned with Chef's predicament. Chef whispered into the receiver and the voice whispered back. Now the voice sounded like John Wayne. It all felt like a dream. Chef was crying. The howling was getting closer. Chef pushed his body against the adjustable doors of the phone booth. He held the drowned *idiota* close.


Wheels sputtered over the gravel, crawling within inches of Chef's face. Hot steam chapped his already blistered lips. He was on his back in the mud. There were cigarette butts scattered on his chest. He rolled over and stood up. He was covered in strange hair. His knuckles were bleeding and as he limped he could see the shattered phone booth glass. The car horn blared. Chef teetered on his good leg, adjusted his pants and tried to give the driver a finger to suck on but forgot which was an insult and which was a precoital proposition. The last thing he needed was to tango with crazed homosexuals on a night like this.

"Hey, soldier!" the driver of the car yelled, pressing on the horn and sending a tornado of noise rattling through Chef's ears. "You need a hand? Don't be shy now!"

Chef didn't answer the stranger. How long had it been? The sky was full of lavender streaks. He didn't hear any dogs.

Words escaped him. He needed the right words. He needed to tell this stranger that he was too busy for shenanigans because he was being a hero. He dragged the drowned man out of the mud, subjecting his leg to more itching and burning.

"Get in, soldier," the stranger said, rolling down the window. "You look like a man in need of being saved."

"Are you the one I phoned?" Chef asked. He glanced nervously behind him. Still no dogs.

"Phone? Hell, I don't believe in them. Not since Nixon. Look, do you want a lift or not?"

"*Nada.*"

"Suit yourself, soldier."

"Wait," Chef said. "The dogs are coming."

"Amen. Get in, soldier."

Chef pushed the drowned man's corpse across the rear bench seat until the feet tucked under the body in an awkward fetal position. He used some of the newspaper on the floor to cover the body. Then he collapsed into the passenger seat. The car sped off.

Chef measured time by the stranger's cigarettes. One. A dozen. Forty-six. He seemed to be doing it to drown out the odor of the dead man in the back seat.

"If you were to look up misery in a dictionary they'd have a picture of your face," the stranger said. He laughed. He was at least a few dozen years older than Chef. He had a bushy black beard. He wore a cowboy hat with a silver band. The veins on his hands looked like railroad tracks. "Tell me your story, soldier," the stranger said.

"I'm busted up," Chef mumbled. "Caught up in some *idiota*."

"Tell me something I don't know. And don't talk crazy. I don't like men that talk like they've been inside the fun house."

Chef cleared his throat. "The body's mine. I found it. I was trying to save it from the goddamn dogs." His head began to clear, the pain drifted, although he could still feel the saltwater and other vermin creeping about and infesting the insides of his leg. He rolled down the window to let the breeze wake him.

The stranger looked at the corpse in the back seat. "Sure, sure," he said. "I wouldn't try to take him from you. I know what it's like to save something. Believe me. I've been in your shoes."

Chef stared at his bare feet. He wasn't sure if that should make him feel relieved or nervous. He still hadn't quite decided if what he was doing was grotesque or divine.

"Name's Chef," he said, shutting his eyes and waving away smoke.

"Gabe Fishmonger. Guess you could say I'm your guardian angel tonight." Chef eyed the stranger nervously. "I know. Idiotic name, right? Goddamn Russian ancestors knew only one English word when they came here. One lousy word so everybody knew what line of work they did. I don't know who's dumber: people that open their mouths to tell the truth or people who close their ears so they don't have to listen. That's

America for you. Get labeled one thing and it sticks with you for this life and the next. Like flies on shit."

The car raced around bends and down hills. The highway became a gray bullet.

"That was our town," Chef said. "We passed it."

"Was, soldier. We're moving on to greener pastures."

"I didn't kill him," Chef said suddenly, jerking his head around to make sure the drowned man didn't fly out the window. The car was really cruising now, vibrating like it might fall apart. Chef worried this Fishmonger was some avenging angel come to drive him out to the middle of nowhere and punish him for his crimes. Or worse, drive him out to the middle of nowhere and take away his chance at heroism.

"Don't apologize. Sometimes a man just needs to be killed."

"Found him in the ocean," Chef said. "Goddamn hero, right?"

"Shit, they don't make men like us anymore," Fishmonger smiled. He bit down on a rusty dog tag hanging around his neck and hacked out a laugh. "The world needs more men of our kind."

"Wherever you're taking us, just make sure the dogs don't follow. There must have been a thousand of them."

Fishmonger said, "Where we're going there is no coming back." Then he laughed. "Don't mind me. I'm just talking crazy."


They must have driven damn near a hundred miles away from the coast. It took hours, maybe days, driving through wasted gray towns that disappeared under endless miles of orange dust. When he was awake, Chef felt as though he was caught in a bad dream and tried falling back asleep. When he slept, he felt trapped in a nightmare and kept trying to wake himself up.

Soon they were the only car on a narrowing road.

At first, Chef thought this Fishmonger was a diabolical Columbus who had driven him off the end of a flat earth, but then he realized it was the desert. He wondered how close they were to Vegas, how close they were to his ex-girlfriend. He wanted to kill Fishmonger for bringing him here, for reminding him. Or maybe this was a chance to make amends. Maybe he could talk to her. Maybe he could show her he was a changed man. He wasn't the same guy who followed her home from the movie theater, or watched her from the skylight as she read cheap romance novels, or came in through her window while she slept and left the bathtub full of flower petals. He was different now. Being intimate with the dead had saved him in a strange way.

Fishmonger's ramshackle house was at the end of a road to nowhere. He said he hadn't lived in it for many years. Collapsed roof. Shattered windows. There was a shed about fifty yards down the slope where Fishmonger said he had all the essentials. They carried bundles of newspaper from the trunk inside the house that was filled floor to ceiling with stacks of newspaper. What wasn't newspaper was junk: cardboard boxes, oily rags, photographs, ribbons, honorary medals, and a television set lying on its side with the screen kicked in and a photograph of a woman taped over the hole. Chef tried to find a good place to sit down. When he did he peeled back the edge of the cast and winced. It smelled terrible.

"Pour some whiskey on that shit," Fishmonger said, tossing him a bottle.

Chef drank. The insides of his head were a melted Ice Age.

"You never told me what happened to the leg, soldier."

"Accident," Chef gargled.

Fishmonger leaned back on the stack of newspaper he was using as a sofa. He sucked in his cheeks. "Nope, nope, nope," he said. "It merely appears to be an accident. It might even appear to be a mystery, but it is fate. We were destined to find each other, you and me. God is a door-to-door salesman of mystery, soldier. We just need the courage to open the door and buy in bulk."

"No," Chef said, patting his broken leg. "Accident. Girl trouble." He thought it best to disagree and leave it at that. There was no telling what this poor *idiota* was capable of.

"You see that car?" Fishmonger said, pointing out the window. There was an old pickup showered in rust. "That was hers. I pay a kid to come once a week to piss all over it. Gives me wood to watch him do it, swear to god. No offense. Sometimes he slashes a tire or uses the crowbar on the windshield. But I prefer it when he pisses. I don't have the courage to do it myself."

Chef looked around the room as if he had heard none of it. "What is it you do?"

Fishmonger let out a deep breath. "Good question. No pity party, you hear? Me? I survive. This place was ours. Was, mind you. She moved on. I live out in the shed. Doesn't smell like her out there. I figure when the time is right the Lord will smite this Gomorrah with a plague."

"What now?" Chef asked, hoping to steer the conversation somewhere else.

Fishmonger stared at the ceiling. There was a long, awkward silence.

"I figure we better wash that body," he said.


Fishmonger had no difficulty pulling the corpse out of the car and slinging it over his shoulder like a deer carcass. They spent the night washing it clean, combing the hair, manicuring the nails, and brushing his teeth. They stripped the corpse naked and pulled the critters out of him with tweezers. Then they dressed him in Fishmonger's Sunday best. Chef knew they had to act fast. He had paid attention in biology class. Decomposition was not something to celebrate.

That night there was a vigil. They put the body in a wicker trunk. They lit candles. Fishmonger offered the prayers and read other passages from the Bible. It was pitiful, but Chef was not about to argue with this *idiota*. His only suggestion was that the drowned man might not have been a Christian so perhaps they should give him all the last rites they could think of, just in case. Fishmonger agreed. They got out a broken trumpet from the attic and took turns trying to play jazz. They shared cigarettes with the corpse. They placed coins over his eyes and in his mouth, but Fishmonger said he needed a beer for where he was going. They put a six-pack in the trunk along with some pieces of stale fried chicken.

They admired the drowned man's hands, the curls in his hair, the religion still impressed in his eyes, and the narcissism in the way he lay there without giving a damn. They wondered how many men he had killed, how many mothers he must have made weep, how many children dreamed of being like him.

"This is no man," Fishmonger said. "This is a fucking constellation. He belongs with his kind in the stars."

Later, they buried him in an unmarked grave not far from a small thicket of trees in a stretch of dust and cactus. Chef smoked and watched while Fishmonger worked the shovel and pickax. It was a shallow grave.

"What a lovely fucking treasure," Fishmonger said. "We are some heroes, right, soldier?"


Gunfire startled Chef out of his dreams and, believing they were under attack, he performed a shitty half-somersault across the shed floor. Pain danced up his leg and into his crotch. Another burst of gunfire, then laughter, and after sufficient silence Chef looked up and saw a shirtless Fishmonger standing over him.

"Here they come," Fishmonger grinned. "The enemy arrives for invasion."

It was coyotes. Dozens of them.

"What do they want?" Chef said. He was nervous. Fishmonger pointed to the unmarked grave among the cactus.

"Isn't it obvious? They've come for the drowned man."

Every time Fishmonger shot a coyote the others skittered off for a few hours. When they returned, Fishmonger shot another and the cycle repeated itself. Vultures descended. Soon their black feathered corpses lay among those of the wounded and dying coyotes. The coyotes snacked on the birds, but mostly they unearthed the corpse bit by bit, digging up a little here and there. It was a little dance. Dig a little, retreat and circle. Dig a little, retreat and circle.

"Amateurs," Fishmonger whispered. He shot a coyote between the eyes.

This far away in the desert every gunshot echoed until the only sound was echoes of echoes. The men kept track of time by monitoring the coyotes. Some internal instinct compelled the creatures to circle back around every sixty-five minutes. It's like they too could not resist the corpse, prisoners to their biology. The more coyotes Fishmonger killed, the more coyotes appeared with the pack the next time. Maybe there were that many coyotes in the desert, or maybe killing them was really bringing them to life. It was like some strange but intoxicating mitosis.

When the coyotes returned they writhed in slow circles, snouts lifted. With every gunshot they scattered and disappeared into the trees or left clouds of dust. Then they charged, dug around the corpse, and ran off before the next shot.

"That dead man is our stewardship. We must not fail him," Fishmonger said as he reloaded the rifle. "Faith binds us. Faith in instinct. Faith that he is dead and must remain dead under the earth where he belongs. Faith to pull the trigger and kill our brother coyotes. Faith that their animal hunger will bring them to us. Faith that my instinct is true. Faith that what we do is honorable. Faith that the circle will continue."

"Jesus Christ," Chef said, "you are a fucking loon."

He thought of escaping, but where would he escape to? And what was to stop Fishmonger from burying him with the drowned man?

After a few days, bits and pieces of the drowned man began to poke through the dust and it seemed as if he was trying to resurrect himself. Flies swarmed and laid their eggs. The coyotes fought for scraps. Fishmonger gathered the tools.

"He must be something holy if they want him so bad." He opened the shed door. "We best bury him again."

Chef watched the crazy old *idiota* walk up the dusty path hauling a bucket of water and a shovel. The coyotes had run off to the trees where they waited patiently. They seemed to understand this was all part of some game of which they were necessary participants. Fishmonger bowed to them, as if he too was enjoying this game.

The two men kicked away coyote carcasses and wrenched free the drowned man. His face had been gnawed up. He looked nothing holy, just a rotten drowned man without any peace in this world or any other.

"The nerve of this sonfabitch to try and be reborn," Fishmonger said. He poured water on the grave to loosen the soil. He started digging a deeper grave. Chef used a bucket to collect stray pieces of the drowned man.

"Leave him. This is his fate. What God has taken we cannot unravel."

Chef ignored him and gathered pieces of the drowned man. He held them gently, wondering if these bone chips were dead man or dead coyote.

"You say I'm sick in the head but here I am trying to bury this poor devil and there you are collecting pieces of him. Who is the diseased and who is the doctor I ask?"

"You need therapy," Chef said.

"Therapy is alright. It can be therapeutic," Fishmonger said.

"You're a masochist."

"I've never believed in the Mormons."

"No, masochist," Chef said.

"Yes, I have good reasons not to believe the Mormons," Fishmonger said, preparing one of his sermons that by now Chef was all too familiar with. "There's a guy up the river, big chap with cankers all around his lips. Each canker's like its own little smile. That's just the way the world is, I suppose: some people have cankers, and others, well, others get washed up on the ocean shore." He aimed for the tree line, fired twice. "So this Mormon fella had a beautiful woman. Curvy. Smelled like fruit. But his business, his true love, was hogs. Best bacon you'll eat this side of the mountain. They eat their young, you know? The hogs, I say, not the Mormons. I don't know what Mormons do for food." Fishmonger lit a new cigarette and continued about how the Mormon cowboy's wife would deliver ten pounds of bacon once a month and eventually they went to bed. "We were happy," he smiled. He fired at the coyotes again. "Then one day she stopped coming. Made me crazy. Looked for her but never found her. It was only later I learned her husband killed her. Butchered her up on the Sabbath. Fed her to his hogs. He still brought me the bacon. For six months I ate the hogs that had eaten her. Never tasted the difference. We loved too much and it cost us both in the end."

Chef stretched inside the empty bathtub. His shit leg hung over the porcelain edge. Fishmonger poured steaming water into the tub. He left the shed and returned with more buckets. He told Chef he needed his strength. He touched Chef's hair. How else would he find romance again? Chef closed his eyes. When he opened them Fishmonger was gone.

The shed was a mess. Old tin containers and rusted forks, buckets of water, bullets on the floors and windowsills, the smell of rubber and piss. There were buckets of bone fragments. There was hardly anything left of the drowned man now but pieces. The game was almost finished.

Chef had promised himself he would gather what pieces he could, as much as he could, remains they could identify, and when he got back to town he would find Fiske's widow or his parents or anybody who knew Fiske and deliver the remains so he could be dead in peace. Somebody had to be looking for him. Somebody was losing sleep. This was no way to die. He just hoped to live long enough to do this one good thing.

Maybe Fishmonger was trying to fool him. Maybe Fishmonger had guessed his plan. Maybe while Chef slept the old man stole the bone fragments and buried them just for Chef to collect them the following mornings, just to keep him here, to keep the game going.

He held the bones between his fingers and used an old rag to clean them. "Apologies, Fiske," he said.

Chef tried to stir his senses: where he was, what he was doing. He did not remember how many days they had passed in the shed. They had pissed in empty whiskey bottles, sometimes forgetting which bottles were whiskey and which were piss. He hobbled to the window, looked out and saw nothing but dust and cactus. Fishmonger's thin shadow in the distance. He was burying the corpse again. Chef aimed the rifle at the old man's throat.

"*Pow*," he whispered.

That night Fishmonger did not return. Chef waited alone, counting the coyotes on the ridge. The next morning Fishmonger was in the shed but the two men did not speak. Fishmonger tossed the pickax and shovel into a corner. Chef went back to work on the new assortment of bones he had collected. Fishmonger seemed disgusted by this. He ate from a can of beans with his fingers.

"They've devoured him," he said. "Nothing but pieces. In time, the Lord will provide a new stewardship. But until then we must make our stand against them. Keep the faith, brother."

That afternoon Fishmonger shot the coyotes and Chef reloaded the rifle. When he looked out the window all he could see were coyotes.

"Jesus, where the hell did they all come from?"

In that moment Chef envied them. They had a brotherhood. They had a purpose. They had instinct. And behind all that there was a sense of heroism in what they did. Either that or it was a whole mess of *idiota*.

Chef hobbled under the stars. The night was idle. With each step sand squirmed between his toes, as if exhausted with this endless charade of beasts. He dropped to his knees after he climbed up the ridge. The shed was a mere thirty yards behind him. The coyotes were close, and when Chef growled they circled closer. Bent on all fours, his hands fumbled in the darkness for pieces of Fiske.

Is that you? he whispered. Where have you gone, amigo? Are you *nada*? Are you *idiota*? he laughed.

Behind him Fishmonger screamed: "Salvation!"

Gunfire echoed. Clumps of dirt sprayed. The old cowboy was crouched in the shed doorway, mostly naked. He reloaded. Jesus. The goddamned crazy was shooting. Chef tried to yell but when he opened his mouth it filled with greedy laughs and howls. Then he howled again until his insides burned, head low to avoid Fishmonger's misfires. The coyotes swarmed, lapping gray tongues on his legs and belly. Chef ignored them. He tore the cast from his leg, exposing the raw flesh, and zigzagged back and forth among the pack. He felt free. He felt for the first time, twisted there on all fours, like he too was *nada*. More gunfire. A coyote head exploded. Chef could hear Fishmonger giggling. A wounded coyote twisted closer in the dark and coughed blood into his lap. As its breathing slowed, an eye blinked and blinked. "Apologies," Chef whispered. Welcome to the *nada*. Welcome to the *idiota*. Chef pawed at the dust, pulling back dark sweeps of tumbleweed and dirt only to discover old copper coins, those they had stuffed into the drowned man's mouth. There were bones, too: scraps of femur and clavicle, even broken teeth. Fishmonger kept firing, kept screaming *Salvation! Salvation!* and Chef clawed at the dust until his fingers bled and he had unearthed Fiske's jawbone. He held it against the soft flesh of his cheek, this lovely mask. Such an *idiota*, he grinned, and laughed heroically as he held on to what remained.

# Everything You Wanted to Know
# About Astrophysics but Were Too Afraid to Ask

Distinguished guests and esteemed members of the society—I thank you for the opportunity to deliver the keynote address at this the 226th meeting of the American Astronomical Society. Many thanks to Michio Kaku for that flattering introduction. As you may or may not notice, I am not Stephen Hawking. My name is Oliver Obermann. Dr. Hawking asked me to speak on his behalf tonight regarding the minor issue of black hole radiation in Bose-Einstein condensates, with which I have a little personal experience. Forgive me if I defer all discussion of the mathematics to the end as I am not very good with numbers. I promise to keep my remarks to a minimum, as Neil deGrasse Tyson has informed me the conference auditorium must be cleared in thirty minutes for the annual meeting of the Association for Pet Obesity Prevention.

I first became aware of the existence of black holes during a speed-dating event last year. I don't need to explain to members of this society the particulars of such an event. It was during speed-date round fourteen that I met Moira. After our third date Moira assured me she was not contagious. She was ill, but there was no reason to be alarmed. She could laugh, cry, kiss, pee, and carry on with her life for now. But her prognosis was bleak. I ran through a list of possible diseases in my head: flu, typhoid, hepatitis, malaria, leprosy . . . *what?* Did she have the plague? I must admit, I was aroused. And a little nervous. Most of the women I date are boring. They have nice teeth and love their mothers. They don't have Moira's wry sense of humor. For an ill person she looked fantastic.

This is awkward, she said. I've never told anyone what's wrong with me.

Go ahead, you can tell me anything, I said, which was an obvious lie because it had only been two dates and I wasn't ready for anything.

Moira confessed she was collapsing. Not from adrenal failure or cancerous growths. This wasn't fatigue. This was not some psychobabble about the disenfranchisement of women within the laboring classes, she insisted. She was collapsing into herself. It's subatomic, Moira said. Gravity is pressing in and thermodynamics is pressing out.

You mean, like science? I wondered. I told her I worked demolition on a night crew.

Moira said that according to her best calculations, the struggle in her body between gravity pulling in and radiation pushing out would shortly end as all her matter collapsed into a concentrated point no bigger than a fleck of dust. It was possible there would be a supernova. But then total blackness. That was her official diagnosis: *collapsarus humanitas singularitus.*

I'm becoming a black hole, Moira said.

You might find it hard to believe, but it is the first clinical observation of its kind.

Later, when we were in bed together, Moira showed me where the black hole had started to form. It was on her shoulder. It looked like a freckle.

That's it?

That's it, she said.

What can I say, my fellow scientists? Black holes are incredibly disappointing.

She said she had an itch one morning. An itch that didn't go away. Then it felt like a lump. She went to the doctor. Her mother had died of cancer. But this wasn't cancer, the doctor said. He didn't know what it was. After reviewing the lab work he told her to consult with a physicist.

Her insurance didn't cover the university hospital, so she ended up at a community college. The physicist was a little annoyed. Then Moira started taking off her shirt and said she was going to show him something he had never seen before. That got his attention and he was less grumpy.

Another round of tests showed that around the freckle was a high concentration of nitrogen and helium and traces of hydrogen cyanide. Star stuff, he called it. What did that mean? Moira wanted to know. The physicist said a black hole was the only logical explanation.

Will it hurt? she asked.

Theoretically? No, the physicist said. You might feel some tearing as space and time stretch. We call it spaghettification.

I like spaghetti, Moira said.

The physicist shook his head and said science is wasted on the wrong people.

I wasn't sure if I believed Moira's story. She was a nice girl, but a black hole? I had dated crazy but nothing like this. Still, it was a fantasy I could not resist.

It's no big deal, Moira told me the next morning as she got on her clothes. Sooner or later we're all eclipsed, right? C'est la vie.

I wasn't sure that was the time to start thinking like the French. While Moira worked at the bakery I wrote a letter to Stephen Hawking.

DEAR MR. HAWKING. I KNOW YOU'RE TERRIBLY BUSY, BUT I HAVE A QUESTION. IT IS A MATTER OF LIFE AND DEATH. IS THERE ANY WAY TO COEXIST WITH A BLACK HOLE? THANK YOU. YOURS IN SCIENTIFIC SOLIDARITY, OLIVER OBERMANN.

I'm happy to report to the society we tried to forget science and make this romance work. Moira and I were inseparable. Our relationship was all light and no shadow. We took walks around town. We kissed in the rain. When I came home from the construction site she was waiting for me and when she came home from the bakery I was waiting for her.

But the seriousness of her condition manifested almost immediately. Nobody else noticed, but I did. It was little things. Her back hunched. Her knees buckled. She complained of heart palpitations and muscle spasms. Customers didn't come to the bakery interested in coffee and orange rolls. No, she was a bottomless pit for all their venting, for all their secrets. I told her I could be her anchor, tethering her to the atomic scaffolding of our lives.

Now, I won't bore you with the math of how black holes consume dust and gas at a rate conforming to Velikov's electrothermal instability theorem, but understand that Moira was no different. She knew her time was limited and she was trying to soak up the world before it slipped away, before it collapsed in on her. She said there was too much. Too many books to read, too much food to taste, too much virtuality to process, too many indigenous tribes not yet discovered, too many cats to save from alleys. It made her head hurt, like when she was five and she ate too much ice cream.

They had it right all those years ago, she said. The world is too much with us. There is too much to know and not enough time.

Despite what the doctors and physicists told her about her painless termination, Moira worried. She had always wanted to be a mother, but not like this. Black holes swallow galaxies. What if I swallow the world? Think about it, she told me as she paced the room. What if this is the end of poverty, chocolate, public libraries, the Electoral College, long walks on the beach? What if we lose it all, Oliver? How can I live with myself if I give birth to that loss?

She punched the wall. It left a hole the size of her fist.

That won't happen, I lied. I won't let it happen.

What can you do, Oliver? What can any of us do?

Now, I know we are men of science gathered here, so I'm a little embarrassed to admit I dabbled in the humanities to comfort Moira. We hugged. I told her there was still time. We could get married. Maybe love is a transformative physics that operates outside the laws of quantum mechanics.

No, it's useless, Moira said. This is all we are now. You stretching one way and me another.

My fellow scientists: that is romance. Sooner or later we'll all be alone, stretched too thin and staring at what used to be the edge of our lives. We just need a physicist to do the math to prove it.

That night we fell asleep together. The next day Moira was gone.

It didn't take long to find what was left of her. I took one look at the hole on the wall and I knew it was her. Her collapsing was complete. Somehow she had not burst into a supernova and swallowed all the pain and love and happy birthdays and goodbyes as she feared. This is the way her world ended: stretched too thin to be anything else but a hole.

I got very close to the hole without being too close. I had read all about the event horizon. I knew my limits. I loved Moira, but I wasn't ready to be a part of her.

The hole emitted no odor. No synchrotron radiation, no nitrogen. No Schrodinger's cat, so somebody tell Polyakov to rescind his paper. It looked very familiar to the freckle Moira had on her shoulder. Moira, I whispered. Moira, can you hear me? Can you understand me? Will you give me a sign it's you? There was an echo trapped inside, almost like a hiccup. I couldn't tell what the echo was saying. It sounded like Moira, but I wasn't sure. The more I listened wanting to believe it was her the more I felt my insides tearing in two directions, hollowing me out like a bowl.

I thought about running out the door and never coming back. Maybe Moira was right. Maybe it was useless. Then I saw the postcard on the countertop. It was from Stephen Hawking. The picture on the postcard was of the Milky Way. The candy bar, not the galaxy, because, if you don't know already, Stephen is a real ass. On the back of the postcard, scribbled in lousy penmanship was the answer to my question.

Dear Oliver. It is theoretically possible, but so is everything.
Best of luck. Stephen.

I decided not to leave. What good would that have done? Sure, you can run away from women, even love, but never science.

I made dinner for the black hole that night. Spaghetti with meatballs. I tied the meatballs to long strings of pasta and tried to throw them inside the hole from the other side of the room. Like fishing. I tried to pretend we were together again, but the future seemed out of reach. There was only the past and the present was being stretched in too many directions. Part of me knew she was not coming back, part of me knew I had to let her go. We had passed the event horizon of our relationship. It was only a matter of time before I would forget. Still, I could not leave her.

I stayed with the hole day and night. I kept it company. I fooled myself into thinking I could make this relationship work. And yes, for those of you already thinking it: there are things you can do with a black hole you can't with a regular woman, but this is hardly the place to discuss such affairs of the heart.

In the beginning the black hole was timid in my presence. She shrunk down to the size of a coin, trying to disappear from my sight. Over time she became comfortable with my presence. She was a marvel, expanding and contracting on a whim, inviting me and refusing me, but always seducing me. She was all echo and void, a bottomless pit who seemed indifferent to me. She was nothing inside—she had no center, no core—but it was always an attractive emptiness, always out of reach, always at the point of something. In a way I am ashamed to admit, I loved Moira more this way—as absence rather than presence.

Other times it was just a hole on a crumbling wall.

Eventually we drifted apart. We were in different spaces now, emotionally more than physically. I had tried to take the relationship to the next level, summoning the courage to walk past the event horizon and crawl inside the hole. My fellow scientists, it was strange. I did not feel myself stretched like spaghetti. I did not feel time stand still on the head of a pin. I could only feel emptiness as it slowly evaporated back into the universe.

When I regained my senses I was lying on the floor. I stared at the hole as it continued collapsing until becoming just another invisible crack on the wall.

When I'm not lecturing astrophysicists on all the things they misunderstand about the universe, sometimes I still work the demolition crew. I like to level buildings. I like to dig foundation pits. Sometimes I just grab a sledgehammer for no reason at all and just start swinging. When I see a crack on the sidewalk I'll wedge a few fingers inside so it does not have to feel so lonely. If I see a rabbit hole I get close to it, wondering if I'll feel Moira's absence. It is all so fragile but nothing I do, nothing any one of us does, makes any real difference. Science will keep being science. Whether it's a pothole in the street or the ozone in the sky, we keep making holes because we want to reach inside them, grasping for lost horizons in a constant search for the other end of nothing.

# Indulgences

Yesterday the doll saw me naked. It's one of those Baby Breathe™ dolls that performs the fluid functions: she belches, cries, sneezes, pisses, shits, and, yes, just like it advertises on the packaging, she breathes. In product development they engineered a menstruating prototype but it was rejected on the grounds of being unrealistic. A pity, really, because the marketing department had partnered with tampon companies on some innovative holiday promotion strategies.

I work for the Company. Inspection division, thirty-eighth floor. All junior inspection specialists have an identical office: padded walls, vaulted ceilings, and hygienic tile floors. A one-way glass window separates me from the conveyor belt. Between me and the window is an emergency chute with tin flaps. Behind me is the curtain. This is the room.

My job is simple. Manufactured Baby Breathe™ dolls arrive on the conveyor belt, one every fifty-two-point-two seconds. This is my protocol: approach the window until standing on the tin flaps. Once positioned, disrobe. Stand naked—arms at side, no sudden gesticulations—until the Baby Breathe™ subject responds with one of fourteen hundred and eighty-seven preprogrammed humanoid responses. When subject exits, clothe, apply lotions as necessary, and wait until new subject enters on the conveyor belt. Repeat process until shift expires.

Nobody is quite certain why a naked man is required for product testing on Baby Breathe™ dolls. Perhaps the chief executive officer is deranged, perhaps her marriage is shabby, or perhaps my superior is actually a committee of fully-conscious Baby Breathe™ automatons wishing to torment their creators. The process is reliable. Lawsuits are down, sales up. Effective dolls are sent to distribution. Defects are disposed. Should I fail to properly perform or deviate from my protocols the tin flaps open and I am disposed down the chute.

It is unusual, such protocols. Is it unusual? I'm not qualified to judge. I am merely a loyal employee.

My shift has continued for five hundred and forty-seven consecutive days. This loophole is possibly a clerical error, but the employee handbook insists there are neither errors nor loopholes.

And so it is: rise and disrobe, rise and disrobe.

Before the Company I performed protocols for the military. My expertise was explosives. After you've seen the human body explode, it both reassures your existence and inspires a career change.

Now I rise and disrobe and Baby Breathe™ dolls arriving on the conveyor belt confirm my existence through one of fourteen hundred and eighty-seven preprogrammed humanoid responses. Once we have completed our protocols we continue on the conveyor belt of life.

The problem with yesterday is the sigh. Baby Breathe™ dolls are not programmed to sigh, and certainly not with such melancholy.

Ergo, the sigh came from Ms. Vox.

Ms. Vox is the woman behind the curtain. She controls the incinerator chute. I have no proof she exists and no knowledge of her protocols, but all protocols dictate a fail-safe option. I imagine she is middle-aged, left-handed, divorced, prefers

Bach to Stravinsky, speaks in a stilted amphibian tone, and likes to be handled by men in bathrobes. Instinct tells me Ms. Vox is the president of the Baby Breathe™ Company and the dolls are patterned in her likeness. I have faith in this. I would like to believe we are part of something larger here, something consequential, something more than conveyor belts and protocols. I am not supposed to know that Ms. Vox exists, assuming she does exist, and yet I have faith even right now she is thinking of me thinking of her on the other side of the curtain. Perhaps we cannot exist without our hope of the existence of the other, even if entertaining such thoughts means subjecting ourselves to the incinerator chute.

How often I have stood naked on the thirty-eighth floor devising protocols to confirm my existence to a hypothetical Ms. Vox.

I could press the yellow button. It is behind a pane of glass next to the door. Pushing the yellow button sends the signal. What signal? I do not know. Is this unusual? Maybe. Pushing the yellow button is not my protocol. And I am a loyal employee. Perhaps once pushed the world will vanish. Perhaps the Baby Breathe™ dolls will take over the world. Perhaps pushing the yellow button will free Ms. Vox from her protocols. I have reason to believe that behind her curtain Ms. Vox waits to press an almost identical yellow button which controls the incinerator chute on which I stand. She may only press the yellow button if I disregard my protocols. That is her protocol. We are opportunists, me and Ms. Vox, verifying the other's existence through the threat of annihilation.

Yesterday was the first time in five hundred and forty-seven consecutive days that I almost pressed the yellow button. After disrobing for a Baby Breathe™ doll nothing happened. A defect. Only this defect remained on the conveyor belt staring at my defective nudity. Panicked, I defied protocol and placed my finger on the yellow button. Then I heard the melancholic sigh.

And here we are, caught in our loophole.

The only logical explanation for the melancholic sigh is love. Neither Ms. Vox nor I have ever verified one another's existence, our interactions are hypothetical, but love demands nothing less than an absurd series of protocols.

So I wait in my loophole. It makes a lovely equation, the mathematics of our love. In time it will become chemistry, which must become physics. This is the order of things. For now, I must wait for Ms. Vox to solve her end of the equation.

Every day I would like to throw back the curtain and disrobe passionately for whatever is waiting behind the curtain. I would like to be stunningly naked and risk reciprocity, even if causality entails the incinerator chute due to my own defects. Though, I suspect love is better this way: rise and disrobe, rise and disrobe, each of us behind our respective curtains. Better to remain suspended in anticipation, to submit to the protocol loophole, to wait for the next unexpected sigh, to remain subject to the irresistible charms of displaced indulgence.

## Ellie's Brood

The turkeys were Harvey's idea. He remembered what one of the old-timers said thirty-five years ago when he first purchased the old Sheasby house: to keep from going loopy in the foothills it is best to make friends with the animals. Good country thinking. Over the years Harvey had tried befriending squirrels and wolves and the occasional deer, but his first real animal friend was a woman he managed to get pregnant.

Ellie didn't hold it against him when he joked about it in his weekly newspaper column. PREGNANT CRYPTID CAPTURED AT SHEASBY FARMS—TWO DOLLARS TO PET! was his headline. Neighbors talked. How could Harvey, well, *you know*? Does intercourse still work when there's a thirty-year age difference? You think you know somebody and then, poof, you never know people. Ellie had trouble keeping track of all the rumors. She was a whore, a saint, the victim of predatory male courtship. On more than one occasion the rumor was she had been abducted and impregnated by aliens. And Harvey? He loved the publicity. *What can I say?* he wrote in his column. *It's a savage world in the foothills. Hibernating bears like to stay close to their honey.*

Then the news nobody anticipated.

*Miscarriage,* Harvey reported. *No sympathies, please.*

So, to make Ellie forget the miscarriage Harvey purchased a dozen turkeys. A mix of toms and hens. Fair price from George Lindquist. Cute little devils. Ugly, but cute. He was driving home with them in the back of the pickup when two of the birds took an unfortunate leap and gobbled their way under the wheels of a passing semi. Harvey spent an hour gathering the remains off the highway.

"It's okay," he told Ellie as he unloaded the pickup and sent the remaining turkeys sprawling into the fields. "This makes a baker's dozen."

"You're not a baker," she said coldly. "And you can't count."

"You're missing the point."

Ellie chewed her lip. "What makes you think you can breed wild turkeys?"

"Maybe I can't. But it's something to take our mind off things," he said, trying to be reassuring.

"What *things*?" she hissed. She said it deliberately to make him feel uncomfortable. It hurt her, this flippancy, this old patronizing wisdom of believing he could make it right with the snap of his fingers, even if he wasn't trying to be mean and was only trying to show he loved her. Hey, honey, you lost the baby but I got you turkeys! That was the problem with Harvey: he loved so big he never realized when he was being a fool.

"We need to relax," he smiled, and put his arm around her awkwardly in a half embrace she did not return. With Harvey it was all whimsical. He had avoided seriousness for most of his life. Even when his mother died he turned it into a joke, refusing to give a eulogy and inviting people to the pulpit to tell a story about Judith that made them laugh instead of cry. Harvey didn't make any room for tragedy. That was why he wrote a silly column for thirty-five years and never once said anything worth repeating.

"Breeding them won't be so difficult," Harvey said as they surveyed the turkeys from the slope. No sooner had he said it than he let his chin drop against his chest, the way he did when suffering indigestion. "I did not mean that," he said.

"I know with you it's just words," Ellie said, patting his cheek.

Harvey gazed at the flock which began to sputter and zag in the evening snow. The bigger toms were marking their territory. "Ten is luckier than twelve. I feel good about having ten," he said.

"They're heading for the thicket," Ellie said. "Boy. You sure did get the wild ones."

Harvey snorted. Then he brushed past her. Ellie held her breath as he started into a trot, waving his arms and calling after the turkeys.

Halfway down the butte he was in full sprint. Two of the jakes disappeared into the thicket. Harvey managed to keep the others at bay by throwing snowballs until they started back up the slope toward the old barn that must not have been used in half a century.

After he corralled them into the barn Harvey found Ellie inside. She kissed him on the cheek. Before turning up the stairs she said, "Next time, try not to dream so big."


Harvey converted the barn into a pen for the toms and jakes. On the other side he put up some wire meshing for the gobblettas, as he called them. When he bought the feed and supplies one of the farmers had told him to keep the toms and hens separate.

"Nothing like delayed gratification to raise a roost," Harvey laughed.

"Don't be a jackass, Harvey. If you let those toms on her now they'll tear her to pieces. And I mean pieces. You'll lose the whole rafter."

Harvey stood there with the bag of feed slung over

his shoulder, nodding his head without a clue. The farmers snickered. They knew Harvey never did mind looking like a fool.

"Well, I appreciate the advice," he told them. "It shouldn't come as any surprise that I do my best sex scenes with a typewriter and a glass of gin."

He never could keep the turkeys penned up for long. They were always escaping. Sometime past midnight Harvey could hear the jakes pecking at the windows. When he opened the door they invited themselves inside and stood in the parlor, bobbing and fanning tails as if it were a game.

During the afternoon, when he was tired of writing or bored with reading, Ellie found him in the barn teaching the toms how to gobble. Like the town, they were confused by the winter that refused to thaw.

"If they don't learn to gobble the hens won't know it's time to mate," he explained.

After a few weeks of training Harvey became impatient and decided to let the turkeys roam instead of cooping them in the barn. For two days it seemed to be working. They heard gobbles before sunrise. The toms were strutting like he had read about in the manual and there were other proper courtship displays.

Then one morning they found four of the turkeys butchered during the night. Feathers and guts and turkey heads all down the slope.

"Maybe wolves," Ellie said.

The surviving turkeys seemed to sense something was wrong. For Ellie it was plain to see these were not dumb birds. There was something human about the way the turkeys marched in ritual fashion among the tattered corpses. Circle left. Circle right. Fluffle and ruffle. Gobble gobble. An unsettling little dirge. It gave Ellie hope that nature knew what it was doing even when it seemed to be spiraling this way and that inside her own body.

Harvey was collecting the turkey innards when he noticed one of the toms went into a frenzy. It dashed down the slope, heading for the pond.

"Suicide!" he yelled.

He tried to get Ellie's attention but she was petting one of the gobblettas with purple caruncles and acted as if she didn't hear him. Harvey tossed the half-frozen entrails at her feet as he ran past her.

The tom had leaped into the pond. It wasn't moving. Harvey leaped in after it. By the time he reached the bird it was floating on its side, mostly submerged in the water. Rolling out of the water Harvey took off his shirt and wrapped it around the tom. It still wasn't moving. He tipped it upside down and began to whack it with an open palm. He shook it by the feet.

"Goddamn it! Goddamn you!"

Ellie, who had come out of her trance, watched him swing the turkey by the legs as if it was a wet towel. He whirled it around his head. Twice he rubbed it violently against a tree trunk. He massaged the turkey's chest with his palms. The gobbler's head knocked against his mouth. Harvey tasted blood. His knees buckled under him and, in frustration and rage for fifty-seven years of futility, he tossed the gobbler into a heap of snow like an Olympian. Then he rested with his hands on his knees, trying to catch his breath.

The turkey lay in the snow for a few minutes. Then it twitched. It wobbled back to its feet. It strutted up the slope. It paused in front of the gobblettas to puff its chest and shake its wattle.

"I'll eat you, I'll braise you in your own juices you . . . you . . . *motherfucker!*" he screamed.

Ellie could not stop laughing. Harvey huffed past her, grunting like a school boy embarrassed he's fallen off the playground swings.

Harvey took a long bath. Later, he sat on the bed and watched Ellie alternate between painting her toenails and folding unused baby clothes. She put them in a box destined for the attic. He wanted her to be bitter. He wanted some acknowledgment of discomfort, some forbidden rage. But she kept appearances with a remarkable indifference, with what he supposed could only be the evolutionary legacy of some pioneer stoicism. She was the most audacious toe painter in history.

Maybe this was her way with grief. It wasn't like he knew her *that* well. He had seen her in a window display one afternoon while shopping for some replacement parts for his typewriter. She said she was a professional mattress sleeper.

"If I buy this bed do you come with it?" he asked.

She might have found him creepy if he didn't have such a stupid grin on his face. Like it was his first pickup line in thirty years.

He thought it would be over within a month. It had been four years.

Harvey wrapped his arms around Ellie and pulled her close. He put one ear to her belly. He had not done this when she was pregnant and now he felt like he had missed out on one of life's great mysteries. All these years he had been waiting for something to happen, something, well, dazzling was the only word that came to mind. He thought Ellie would sweep him off his feet, but after four years they were just Harvey and Ellie, Ellie and Harvey. Wasn't there something more? Isn't that what people come out here for? he wondered. To be dazzled? By suicidal turkeys? Nope. He knew better. People retreat to the foothills to be bored. Now he knew why. It was too exhausting to be dazzled.

She ran fingers through his hair. For a moment she thought he might touch her like before. Harvey had little interest in sex. It was a freak of nature she had gotten pregnant at all. Sure, they had a routine, but it was nothing fancy. Like washing dishes.

"I'm fifty-seven next month," Harvey said. "Jesus was in his thirties when he saved the world. What the hell have I done in fifty-seven years?"

Ellie smiled and kissed the top of his head. "You resurrected a turkey."

With the snow momentarily thawed, the toms started mating regularly. At night Ellie could hear them. Harvey was pleased. The hens were really coming into lay. The first breeding yielded nine poults. They matured unreasonably fast. In six short weeks the male chicks had grown into jakes and were trying to mate with their mothers. And then the gobblettas were roosting again. Harvey counted the eggs. Forty-seven.

"It's not natural," Ellie told him as they watched the jakes try to woo their mothers away from the older toms. While one of the toms was busy gobbling to attract a mate, the faster jakes would mount the hen who had answered the call. Then the old tom, entirely oblivious, would mount her a second time. They watched this deranged family charade repeat for hours.

"It's incest," Harvey said, doing his best to sound stoic. "Or some other polygamy."

By the end of the week there were over one hundred eggs in the barn.

"Come to bed," Harvey told her one night as she stood by the door. "It'll even out. Let nature run its course."

For the next two weeks he tried to hide from her the nastiness of the hatching, worried she didn't have the stomach for it. On the other hand, maybe she wouldn't be upset. Since they had been together she had about as much passion as a doorknob.

One morning he found her in the bathroom. She was kneeling among the hens. There was fresh hay in the tub and cracked eggs in the sink. At least four dozen chicks. Chirping and echoes. Bloody handprints on the floor. Soiled towels. Mangled lumps of poult flesh on the tile.

Ellie was bent over one of the smashed eggshells. It was only after she looked at him that he realized she had been giving a newborn poult mouth-to-mouth. The thing squirmed between her fingers like a cannoli. Harvey watched as she took a knife from her pocket and delicately nicked the throat before fitting in the straw. She blew hard. The poult's chest puffed like a sad balloon.

Harvey dropped the egg he was holding.

"Get the fuck out!" Ellie screamed.


Exactly forty-three poults survived the hatching. Most of those in the barn froze to death overnight. They brought the survivors inside. They were ugly, misshapen things. Three beaks, eleven toes, wattles dangling from their asses. They kept breeding. Eighty. Then well over one hundred and fifty turkeys. Harvey lost count. Ellie ran out of names.

Ellie insisted on keeping the turkeys inside. Harvey had grown tired of the affair. He wanted them gone. He was less playful at breakfast, not as quick with his jokes. Ellie suggested he start writing his column again but Harvey said he had lost his appetite for words.

Harvey tried to get rid of the turkeys. He wouldn't say

whether this was for his benefit or hers. He sold as many as he could to restaurants and chased others into the woods. He left the windows open for them to wander outside but not even the wolves could keep pace with the breeding. For every ten butchered by wolves another two dozen hatched. He stopped feeding them, hoping the numbers would taper off. Instead, they ate their own dead.

The turkeys kept them awake at night. When Harvey turned in bed Ellie was waiting for him. She had watched the turkeys breed. She had taken notes, even drawn pictures. It was all very educational. She slept naked now, surprised at her own insistence at trying to be a mother. When Harvey told her to be quiet and tried to fall back asleep she gobbled into his ear before mounting him.

He rolled over one night and was surprised not to find her in bed. He checked the bathroom and the kitchen. All he found were a few stray turkeys roaming the hallways and others asleep in the tub. He searched the barn but she wasn't there either.

Outside, she had left an obvious trail to follow. He went at a casual pace, not wanting to excite himself. How many times had he warned her about these trails? At least a dozen. She wasn't familiar with these woods. It was easy to get lost. And there were salt wells. One misstep and she would be pickled sixty feet deep with nobody to hear her screaming.

Harvey kept pushing through the trees, determined to follow what sounded like gobbling. When the gobbles quieted he followed the thucking of an ax in a tree stump until he found Ellie and her brood.

It was a massacre. Ellie was standing on the far end of a clearing. She wore pajamas stained with blood. Dozens of turkeys circled her like enthusiastic disciples. They turned to look at Harvey, heads bobbing, but Ellie did not. She breathed deeply. She focused on the ax, swinging it like a blind executioner until there was nothing left of the turkey but a clump of feathers and twisted knots of skin. She tossed the remains into a heap and waited for the next turkey to take its place. Good God, Harvey thought, she must have led them out here like the pied piper.

When she paused, Harvey admired the scene. The blood made a handsome drizzle on the snow, cruel and jagged in some places and almost lovingly geometrical in others. He knew she had been at her task for some hours because the snow had fallen unevenly and the spatter of blood beneath the snow emerged in various shades. The earth was a gruesome layered cake. He could not help but feel impressed—unnerved, but deeply impressed by this brutality.

"What are you doing?"

Ellie didn't look at him. He took the ax from her. He did it gently, so as not to startle her.

"I think they're dead," she said. She used a sleeve to wipe her nose. Blood smeared across her cheek. Behind them, the turkeys gobbled.

"What are you doing?" he asked again.

"This is what I do," she said. "This is what I'm made for."

"Come on," Harvey said, a bundle of nerves and sadness. "Let's go home."

She led the way out of the woods. The front door of the house was locked. In his hurry, Harvey had forgotten his keys. All the lights were on inside and it sounded like a cocktail party. Harvey cupped his hands against the window glass. Ellie did the same. It was difficult to make out the shape of things at first, but within a few minutes they could see the silhouetted figures of turkeys. There were hundreds of them.

It was a mess. There was hay. There was shit. There was blood. They had torn open the cardboard box of baby clothes Ellie left on the stairwell, leaving onesies and burp cloths mangled on the floor. One of the turkeys had stuffed its head inside a mitten and walked in circles bumping into furniture. Several toms had violently mated with the hens. There were broken eggshells. Quite a few turkeys were seated around the dinner table.

"You should write about this in the column," Ellie finally said, trying to restrain her disbelief. "People want to know about this kind of thing."

"Nobody would believe it. It's too weird," Harvey said.

Harvey tried the doorknob. It was locked. He tapped the window glass. When Ellie put her arms around him he flinched. She held him. She tried to calm him. For the moment neither of them moved, blanketed by the snow that all around them became a fuzzy, almost blue weirdness drowned out by turkey gobbling. They watched, on the outside looking in, as if it were the first time.

# What the Body Does When It Doesn't Know What Else to Do

The events which led to my curious position at the department of public polling began during election season when the seven-term mayor, in order to prevent fraud, instituted the new policy of staining the thumbs of voters with phosphoric dye. One man, one vote, he said.

I had very little understanding of politics. I knew nothing of polls. I lacked accounting skills, but I was talented with imaginary numbers. I was mostly suited for work that involved raising eyebrows or gesturing puzzled expressions, poorly equipped for professions involving human empathy, such as the time I worked as a florist and suggested to a middle-aged man he would have better luck throwing himself from the bridge than growing begonias. A few days later I read his obituary in the newspaper.

My only real talent was in alchemy. Sadly, the market had been depressed for years.

As a child I had been enamored with solutions. To encourage this curiosity my parents purchased a chemistry set. After creating an indestructible bubble, causing eggshells to disappear, and generating enough static electricity to kill a colony of mice living beneath the floorboards, I considered myself an amateur Faustus. I toyed with transmogrification and came close to discovering the universal solvent.

My greatest success came when I combined a certain genus of flower with a honeysuckle and ammonia solution which, when ingested, induced indifference. I tested it with remarkable success on cats.

My experiments alarmed my parents, concerned I might grow up into one of those people written about in history textbooks.

I tried for years to create an invisibility ink which would afford me a reprieve from human interaction, but only succeeded in creating an ink which left an irreversible stain. I sold my invention to the government and squandered the earnings. Defeated by the chemical world, I took a position as an apprentice at the local confectionery where I wrapped candies.

On Election Day, Mayor Bremmer proudly displayed his stained thumb and then gave an impromptu speech, waxing eloquent on the plight of the working man whose labors made him alien to his own body. Later he came to see us at the confectionery shop. The mayor was known to have a sweet tooth.

The mayor shook my hand. I handed him some butterscotches because I knew they were his favorite.

"You might need these," I said. "To celebrate."

The crowd of constituents cheered when the mayor emerged from the confectionery, a bit wobbly, displaying his severed thumb. He held it high above his head. It was green with phosphoric dye. Apparently, the thumb had been severed while reaching into the machinery that processed the butterscotch candies.

The mayor waved his severed thumb. "The people united!" he shouted. It was his campaign slogan.

Later that night I sat in the doorway and watched as many celebrated the mayor's landslide victory. The confectioner, a man named Ernst, marched with the crowds as a guest of honor, waving his whisk like a magician's wand. In the frenzy of confetti and kissing and idiotic imitation of our political figures, half a dozen people lost their thumbs in various accidents. Applause erupted from the crowds. Two children were hospitalized after mistaking thumbs randomly discarded in the gutter for butterscotch candies.

While the medics tended to the children I began to poll the crowd informally on the likelihood the children survived. One of the parents said that if I was asking such questions I must have intimate knowledge of the affair.

"You don't have an inked thumb," one of the men said.

This was true.

"He doesn't believe in voting. Perhaps he prepared the candies," one of the fathers said.

He informed the police who approached me: "You poisoned the children with candy?" they said.

They brought me before a judge: "So, you're the anarchist?" he said, shuffling through the papers.

As a firm believer in democracy, I remained silent on the charges. I passed a few years in jail reflecting on the situation and determined that politics and alchemy were not distant bedfellows. Perhaps politics was the proper vocation to avoid grief in my employment and find purpose in my aimless existence.

I was released once the children had recovered.

"You were fortunate," the authorities said. They warned me not to encourage any malfeasance.

A new election cycle was underway. I immediately found a position in the department of public polling. I was given an office cubicle and several bubble grids attached to a clipboard. I was told to find solutions. My supervisor was a husky fellow who harbored a profound affection for data. *The polls have all solutions!* he was fond of saying.

I was assigned to the mayor's reelection campaign. I knocked on doors asking such questions as "Do you have a favorable or unfavorable opinion of the water supply?" or "If God exists, do you approve or disapprove of his handling of animals?"

Once finished, I spent the rest of the day at my cubicle looking nervously over the data, pursing my lips and raising eyebrows in notorious fashion. I felt very qualified for the position, having never voted either for or against anything in my life, the epitome of indifference.

The mayor's opponent was a legless man in a wheelchair named Horst who had made his fortune in manufacturing. Plastics, I believe. He was a war veteran. At rallies he spoke of budget deficits and the need for bureaucratic layoffs. He spoke of his hatred for government.

"If the eye wanders, pluck it out. If the hand offends, cut it off," he said. "Government is a body that needs to be disciplined."

People loved his speeches.

The mayor was nervous because Horst had no legs. Voters loved that kind of vulnerability. All the mayor could display was a measly prosthetic thumb.

"Of all the luck!" the mayor lamented, biting his fake thumb. "Damn it! I should have gone to war."

Not satisfied with the loss of his legs, candidate Horst promised to eliminate his own position if elected. "There is no need for a mayor," he shouted to the crowds. "Man can self-govern! We must eliminate the waste!" This was his campaign slogan. Very catchy.

To prove his seriousness on the matter, candidate Horst accidentally inflicted on himself an aneurysm three months before the election. He remained in a coma. There was a vigil where his campaign aides vowed to keep his name on the ballot.

"Because democracy deserves better than another political pessimist," they said.

The crowds cheered.

"It's a touchy situation," the mayor told the press. "When you run against a comatose man you're limited as to what you can say."

The day after Horst slipped into a coma Mayor Bremmer approached my cubicle. I tried to appear anxious while surveying the recent poll data. He stood there for a good while before mustering the courage to look me in the eye. "Horst will win the election," he said. "People love a man in a coma."

"Yes," I said. "The polls indicate favorable results."

"He's promised to cripple the department. We'll all be out of a job."

"What can we do?" It was the kind of thing you say to act sympathetic when you really do not give a damn, but Bremmer's face twisted with a pensive grimace.

"I think it's best if I eliminate my position," he said in a sobering voice.

"That's brilliant," I said without hesitating. It was alchemical. It was the solution we had been searching for. I'm not sure why I was so eager to eliminate Mayor Bremmer. He had never wronged me. He had sacrificed his thumb for the people. I had always considered him a mentor.

After consulting the polls I advised him on which liquids to mix together that would induce elimination.

The next day Mayor Bremmer was not in his office. He missed a luncheon the following afternoon. Then one morning we arrived and the papers from his desk were scattered on the floor and the windows were smashed. There was blood on the carpet. We peered through the shattered window and could see workers from the Department of Sanitation washing away a dark stain on the asphalt.

We announced the mayor's elimination. Some received the news with relief, others with surprise. Horst's campaign scoffed at these dramatic tactics.

"Imitation is a cheap form of flattery," Horst's chief of staff told the press. "We have the only candidate with a vision for the future. The best the establishment can offer the public is an eliminated man."

We published an obituary. The burial was a grand affair. Bremmer's popularity, now that he had eliminated himself, surged in the polls.

Imagine our surprise when less than a week before the election we arrived to find Mayor Bremmer in his old office. His hair was disheveled, his pants wrinkled, and he did not wear his signature blue tie. It was Bremmer and it was not Bremmer.

The staff was fascinated. Why was Bremmer so relaxed and pleased with himself? Had he eliminated weight? Had he redistributed his fortune? Or did he eliminate doubt and discover God?

"Have you spoken with Bremmer?" his secretary asked. "He seems like a different man."

"That's not Bremmer," I said, still in disbelief. "Bremmer has been eliminated."

"Then who is it?" She looked confused.

I shrugged.

I observed Bremmer most of the afternoon. He reviewed the recent poll data. He answered his phone but conversed only briefly. Mostly he scribbled in ledgers. When I decided I could avoid it no longer I went into Bremmer's office.

"Welcome back, Bremmer," I smiled.

He did not acknowledge me. After scribbling numbers and other data in one page of ledgers he proceeded to the next. I was envious of his skill but also his dexterity with a pen. His hand left long, brilliant brushstrokes on the page.

"Kraus wanted me to deliver these," I said. "He thinks you'll approve of your recent position in the polls." I offered the stack of papers.

"No thank you," Bremmer said. "I've eliminated my position."

"We need to formulate a strategy, sir. The election is in less than a week. The press will wish to speak with you. Given the circumstances, the public demands answers."

"The public can demand nothing of me," he said. "I've eliminated my position."

"What about your family, sir?"

"My family understands I have been eliminated."

"Very well," I said, trying to maintain my composure. "There is only one problem, sir: If you eliminated your position, why are you still here?"

Bremmer stopped scribbling in the ledger. He let out one of those exhausted breaths from between clenched teeth. Then he stated very plainly he was an eliminated man, not an imaginary one.

"Will you go on record with that statement, sir? We can consult the polls. Your constituents might find that position favorable."

"That's unlikely," he said. "They know as well as I that I have eliminated my position."

There was no reasoning with him. He was determined to maintain his eliminated condition.

As a parting gift I offered him a butterscotch candy. He kept it on his desk while scribbling in the ledger.

"It must be eliminated, sir," I said, nodding at the butterscotch.

He unwrapped the candy and placed it in his mouth. Before I had reached the door a curious thing happened.

Bremmer choked on his butterscotch. His hands went to his throat. He made some faint whistling noises, then fell out of his chair. He did not twitch.

I had no time to react. One minute Bremmer was with us and the next he had been eliminated. My only regret was that I had offered the butterscotch. I had interfered. Yet I told myself this was the respectable thing. If given a second chance I would have encouraged Bremmer's elimination once more.

In a few minutes most of the staff were standing in the doorway trying to get a better look at Bremmer. He lay on the floor like a piece of old chewing gum. The mayor's secretary, a chubby woman named Ketzia, stood at my side. We looked down at Bremmer. Ketzia could not blink.

"We've eliminated Bremmer," she said. She looked very beautiful, in a helpless way.

We later learned when they cut him open for the autopsy they did not find the butterscotch. Apparently, it had dissolved in Bremmer's throat as a last act of elimination.

The following week, as one might expect, Bremmer won the election in a landslide. As the polls clearly indicated, in politics an eliminated man is king.

We were hired as Bremmer's staff in the mayoral offices. Everybody loved Bremmer. His favorability ratings in the polls surged to an all-time high.

About a month later a woman who worked in the division of public accounting made an appointment to speak with me. Apparently people believed I had been close to Bremmer because I was put in charge of handling his calls and given the title *Special Assistant on Matters of the Public Good*. The woman felt that, in Bremmer's absence, I was best suited to consult on her condition.

"What can I do for you?" I said.

"I wish to eliminate my position," she said.

I did what any rational individual would do: I consulted the polls.

And so it began. I never finished any of my work on the public good because there was somebody in town each day who wished to eliminate his or her position. I listened. I consulted the polls. Some were permitted, others were not. I had an obligation to defend and find solutions for the public good.

Those who succeeded in elimination were shortly after elected to various municipal positions. It was an alchemical imperative.

Eventually, I grew tired of consultations with the public. It was exhausting, this empathy. I was Mephistopheles, interpreting the dreams of others with the polls, but I longed to become Faustus. The solution was elimination.

I needed to confirm this hypothesis.

Now that Mayor Bremmer had been eliminated, I put my name on the write-in ballot. The special election is next week. I have scheduled my own elimination. The polls indicate favorable results.

## St. Abelard's Zoo for Endangered Species

They buried three goldfish that month. The first suffered from an unidentified illness. The second committed suicide and the last one drowned. Nobody attempted to explain the phenomena to the children who insisted on formalities and buried each goldfish beneath the eucalyptus tree in a separate ceremony. They wore bright clothing despite their gloomy faces. When she tucked the children into bed on the night after the last funeral, the mother told them there would be no more pets.

She had always been hesitant with animals and the goldfish situation troubled her. Her husband, Mr. K., dismissed this as nerves. Dying was natural. She did not need to be reminded of this detail. After all, she had grown up on a farm where her father raised sheep. When they said grace at the dinner table her father gave thanks for the animal by name as its remains simmered on a plate. She never forgot that and it made her fear for the animals in their care.

"My father was a gentle man," she said, getting undressed and climbing into bed next to her husband, "with a firm hand for killing."

After the debacle with the goldfish, Mr. K. was surprised the next morning when his wife suggested they have a family outing to the zoo.

The children ran from one exhibit to the next. Thomas, their oldest, had a checklist. He observed each animal carefully, found its position on the list, then waited to determine which of the fourteen most common behaviors manifested. He had organized the list himself using an encyclopedia checked out from the library. The girl, younger by two years, looked at the animals briefly, thoroughly unimpressed.

The mother took photographs. She was very precise. She made requests sharply and without malice, insisting on when the children should flatten their shirts, or move a little this way and that, or wipe that smile away in a pinch. She took pleasure in their obedience. When they ignored her she scolded them and moved on to the next exhibit in frustration.

Almost as disappointing for her as the children were the animals. The giraffes kept their backs turned, the hippos never came out of the water, and the bears refused to wake up. The mother tried tossing a few pebbles near the cave where they slept, hoping for an excellent photograph, but the bears did not even flinch. She had hoped for more. Especially the elephant. After all, it was a privilege to be seen. She had read that zoo animals were therapeutic. Something about being caged made them more empathetic, even helped those with degenerative diseases recover from their illnesses. Her doctor had shared with her this information after their last visit. The zoo was his recommendation.

"Which animals?" Mr. K. asked when she told him.

"Tortoises are best," said the wife. "But also wolves, penguins, and gibbons." She wiped away a small spot of dirt from her blouse. It left a stain and was now a total loss.

"They're all monogamous."

Mrs. K. blinked repeatedly, her mouth crinkled. Her husband was a repository of useless factoids. "I suppose that's true."

"That can't be coincidence."

Mrs. K. ignored him and positioned the children for the photograph with the zebras.

"Zombies!" the girl smiled.

"No, *zee-bras*," the mother corrected.

The girl's face soured. "Zombies," she said defiantly.

Mrs. K. licked her fingers and tried to properly comb Thomas's hair. The boy twisted away from her grip, but could not escape his mother whapping the back of his head when the hair stood up. Mrs. K. gave a disappointed glare before resuming her position a few feet away, staring at them through the camera lens. She muttered to her husband that the boy had inherited his stubborn cowlicks.

"If the shellfish is spoiled, then it doesn't matter how talented the chef," she said.

The children forced smiles. They trotted ahead to the next exhibit. The mother sighed. She turned to her husband:

"They're going to remember this all wrong."

The tortoise and wolf exhibits were closed for repairs. It was a virus for the gibbons and the penguins were secluded for mating. One of the zoo attendants suggested the rare feline exhibit. They marched ahead. They saw bobcats and Bengal tigers. Thomas jotted down more notes.

To amuse the crowd, one of the zookeepers lowered into the lion enclosure a large slab of raw meat. It was almost purple in the center and dripped dark blood. Thomas pointed out they had forgotten to remove the zebra skin on one side, but the mother corrected him and said the zoo was not so barbaric and he must be seeing things. The lion sniffed at the meat, then yawned and stretched before heading back into the shade. It let its heavy tongue hang from its mouth as it stared at the family.

"It's not hungry," Mr. K. said, somewhat amused. "Imagine, a real lion, and it's not hungry."

"Why won't he eat?" the girl asked.

"It's a *lioness*," Thomas corrected them. He scribbled, then looked at his sister and then back at the lioness. His sister stuck out her tongue at her brother. The mother said a proper lady keeps her body to herself. When the girl walked ahead the boy kicked her heels and made her trip. The girl complained but Mrs. K. was no longer listening. With sunglasses swallowing her face she walked ahead, muttering how the girl's little bird voice made it difficult to enjoy nature.

The snow leopards were sleeping. The family could see two small cubs. One of the cubs played with the sunlight that came through the trees, enchanted with the shadows. The other cub alternated between licking itself and falling asleep.

"I'm bored," the girl said.

"Can we see it eat something? What if we let him chase the zebra? Will they let us watch it then?" Thomas asked his father who looked at the boy helplessly.

"There will probably be a lot of blood," Mr. K. said.

"Don't be morbid," the mother said.

She swatted at a fly and took the opportunity to comb her husband's hair to one side. When he flinched as her hand came toward him he bumped into her purse and it spilled over the railing into the snow leopard exhibit. Before she had a chance to say anything Thomas was running back to see the lions, shouting, *There will be blood!* Mr. K. mouthed, *I'm sorry,* before starting a brisk walk after the boy. The girl followed, scuffing her feet on the pavement.

Mrs. K. lamented her poor luck. She found her way down a stairwell and slipped past a door labeled DO NOT ENTER. She hoped to find a way inside the enclosure. Thirty seconds. That's all she needed to recover the items from her purse: her good lipstick, tissues, and the her day planner. The rest was expendable. They were easy to spot from the circular observatory walkway that looked down into the enclosure. Thirty seconds. Nothing disturbed. Nobody would see her.

She was gathering her things into her purse when one of the doors leading into the enclosure opened and a fat zookeeper wobbled inside. She did not know what to do so she crouched perfectly still where she was by the pond, hoping the shade of the tree would conceal her.

The zookeeper checked a few valves near the door and was about to leave when he saw her. He squinted.

"I dropped my purse," she said, standing to her feet. She held up the lipstick in her hand and tried smiling.

"Easy, girl," he kept saying. He puckered his lips and made a god-awful clicking noise with his tongue. She flinched and he made the sound louder while cautiously approaching her, a whip suddenly dangling in his hand. She stepped forward and he cracked the whip like one of those men in a Middle Eastern suspense film.

"I'm a person," she said in an unsteady voice.

"Sure, honey," the zookeeper smiled. He made the puckering noise again.

"You can hear me," she said, not believing what was happening. "You understand me, right?"

"Don't think twice about it, sweetheart," he said. "I talk with all the animals."

"But I only came to get my purse!" she said.

Then the whip cracked down on her and before she knew what was happening she had skittered to the other end of the pond, covered in mud. She watched as the zookeeper slowly backed out the door.

It must have been a few hours later when she awoke and heard voices above her. She hurried out of the mud and into the middle of the enclosure. Sun drowned the vision from her eyes but she could vaguely make out her husband and children beside the observatory deck railing. Fingers pointed in her direction. One of the zookeepers, dressed in a white lab coat and holding a clipboard, spoke very seriously with her husband. Mrs. K. fixed her hair and did her best to brush the mud from her clothes. She called her husband's name and he glanced quickly at her, then back at the zookeeper. She waved to her children but they stood glumly, the boy writing down in his notebook and the girl swinging back and forth on the rail.

"Why are there only two cubs?" Thomas asked the zookeeper.

"The mother died giving birth," he said.

"Will the babies die?" the girl wanted to know.

"We can fool them for a while with bottles, but animals are smart. They die without a mother's touch. You don't fool nature for long."

Mrs. K. was admitted to the zoo on October 22$^{nd}$ according to the medical transcript we retrieved from the city archives. The zoo only wanted her detained overnight as a precaution. Strictly observatory, they insisted. Human to animal diseases are not uncommon, they warned.

"She is ill," Mr. K. said.

"So, you admit it?" a lanky, bald man said.

"Of course I admit it. It's no secret," Mr. K. said with less confidence. "She's very ill. She's been seeing a specialist." The men in lab coats scribbled in their notebooks. "When can I see her?"

"I'm afraid that isn't possible."

"The other doctor said her problem is with the skin. She has lesions. The zookeeper said something about she has the skin of a snow leopard. What does that mean?"

"It means your wife exhibits the physiology of a snow leopard."

"Is that your specialty?"

"Heavens no," the bald zookeeper said. "I'm an expert on whales."

"Then why are you here?"

"For your wife, of course."

Mr. K. stood. He had never learned how to be imposing when he needed to and this moment he wished he could be different. He was a carpenter, good with his hands but slow with words. His wife was the wordsmith. It was one of the reasons he loved her. She would have said something clever. She would have saved him from this indignity. The room was air-conditioned and there were goose bumps on his arms. He thought he should make a scene, but then what would be the point? The children slept on a sofa on the other side of the room. He had not been able to explain to them what was happening, and he wasn't sure he could if he needed to.

"We can address this with the family doctor," Mr. K. said, running his hands through his hair.

"We're all doctors," the whale expert said. "Highly qualified for her condition, I might add."

Mr. K. sat back down and let out a sigh of frustration. "What condition?"


Nobody other than the veterinarian staff was allowed to see Mrs. K. during the first month of evaluation. The zookeepers assured the husband they were performing necessary diagnostics. Once each week, after the visitors had left for the evening, they let her into the snow leopard exhibit for exercise.

The first few days she was belligerent. Her curses were

so foul it made the scientists blush. When she realized her screams were pointless she was overcome with terror and begged them to let her see her husband. She ran from one end of the enclosure to another, trying to open doors and scale the eighteen-foot walls. She cried. She climbed up the tree but only succeeded in annoying the cubs who had taken refuge from her wild display of emotion. When she exhausted herself for the evening she washed her face in the pond, fixed her hair, then brushed the mud from her clothes and asked to be returned to the air-conditioned lab.

She attempted to escape several times. On one occasion, she created a ladder from broken tree branches and almost reached the edge of the wall before the makeshift structure broke and she injured her leg. She limped for weeks. The zoo-keepers remained in the circular walkway above the enclosure and took notes.

She washed her clothes once each week and put on her makeup each morning. If she was going to be treated like an animal, she would look damn good doing it. She discovered that on especially humid days the water from the pond acted like hairspray and she could give herself cute hairstyles. She talked to herself—about life on the farm as a child, her wasted college years, vacations her husband had failed to take her on, and which animals at the zoo were mistakes of God and which were enchanting. At night, she memorized the pattern of stars. She felt that speaking aloud was her only hope at convincing the zookeepers of their mistake. After two months, she quit trying.

When they lowered meat into the enclosure, she was not as fast as the cubs. The first time she approached it hesitantly, then, once she realized what it was, criticized the staff for not having the decency to leave a bottle of red wine.

She watched the cubs eat for days. When she could no

longer endure her hunger, she snatched the morning meal before the cubs were even awake. She stared at the meat for a long time, wondering what to do. She tried to cook it using the mirror from her makeup kit and some leaves but it was a failure. She resigned herself to raw meat. After three days, it spoiled.

When the cubs challenged her prize, cornering her on the shaded end of the pond, she accidentally wet herself. This alarmed the cubs and they sulked away hissing. She later discovered that flecking menstrual blood was more effective at securing her territory.

In the beginning, she was deliberately cruel to the cubs, using rocks and sticks to drive away their curiosity. Within a few weeks, however, when she realized they were her only companions, a natural affinity emerged. She led them to the pond and showed them where to find the coolest water on humid afternoons. When they got ticks, she clawed them out with her nails. When the file from her purse broke, she discovered, much to her surprise, that her teeth were more efficient.


Mrs. K. was washing her clothes in the pond one evening when she saw her husband leaning against the rail on the observatory deck. Beside him were the zookeepers with their clipboards. She waved, hurrying to put back on her damp shirt. She fixed her hair and waved again. She kept calling his name.

Mr. K. turned away with the zookeepers.

Later that night when they delivered her ration of meat, they told her she could leave. There had been a terrible mistake and they were almost certain she was not a snow leopard and no danger to civilization. There was nothing to fear. They apologized for her detainment, but stressed that even though science has its flaws it is the best system available.

Crouched beneath the tree, Mrs. K. stared at the fallen leaves without blinking, gnawing on the meat whose juices dribbled down her chin.

Two months passed before the zoo reopened the rare feline exhibit. The newspaper ran a full article. Mr. K.—the only name ever used in the interviews—had approached the editor with the details of his wife's situation. The editor showed little interest.

"I'm not printing that. We report facts, not fantasies," he had said.

"I know it sounds ridiculous," said Mr. K., "but it's the truth."

The editor was a very large man whose presence inside a zoo cage would not have been suspicious. He lit a cigarette and combed fingers through his thinning hair. He shook his head. "I can't help you. The problem is too many people will believe it."

Mr. K. brought his children to the reopening. None of the other zoo visitors seemed interested in the exhibit and those who did were not alarmed by the wife's presence. They took photographs and moved on.

When the zookeepers lowered the slab of meat, the two cubs kept still under the tree while the mother circled. Blouse in tatters, skirt ripped, hair mud-spackled. Like a castaway on Crusoe's island.

Satisfied with sniffing the meat, she dragged the carcass under the acacia trees and cleaned it before distributing equal portions. One of the cubs tried to steal a scrap and the mother whacked it with an open palm until the cub cowered in the ditch. It whimpered there until the mother made a guttural noise and it rejoined them. The mother stretched the animal on its back and rubbed its belly furiously. While the cubs gnawed on the carcass, the mother licked the dried blood and marrow from her fingers.

"Do they let Mom kill it herself?" Thomas wanted to know.

"Do they think Mom is one of the zombies?" the girl asked.

"That's not your mother," Mr. K. said.


At school, Thomas bragged about his mother the snow leopard. His quarterly theme detailed the dietary needs and evolutionary development of the *Panthera uncia*. He stood in front of the class and described the social behaviors of snow leopards as well as their mating rituals. He presented diagrams. This earned him a trip to the principal's office where he refuted claims he was lying about his mother. He showed them photographs.

The next day Mr. K. joined the boy at a meeting with the vice principal and guidance counselor. They asked Thomas questions but he refused to answer. When they told Mr. K. the boy had tried to lick one of the girls in his class he shook his head. He looked every bit the disheveled single father. Puffy eyes betraying a lack of sleep. Facial hair more beard than stubble.

"What were you trying to do, son?"

"I didn't want the other boys around her. I wanted to mark her," Thomas said in a low voice.

"Women are not sexual possessions, Thomas," the guidance counselor cautioned.

"I'm in heat," the boy replied. He gritted his teeth.

"You're not a snow leopard, Thomas," the guidance

counselor said. She put her hand on the boy's shoulder and he sprang out of the chair like an acrobat, swiping at her with his hand and knocking the glasses from her face in one fluid motion. He hissed from the corner of the room.

"Hissing doesn't make you an animal, it only makes you look like an idiot," the counselor said, putting back on her glasses and giving Mr. K. a petulant stare.

Thomas breathed deeply then let out a loud cry before fleeing the room.

At home, his behavior grew more and more erratic. He roamed the halls at odd hours and spread out on the stairwell to nap. He ignored his homework and chased sunlight. He practiced his pounce. At dinner, he requested raw meat, and when Mr. K. told him to eat his goddamned pasta primavera and like it, the boy growled before shitting on his plate. He quit sleeping on the bed that night and within two days had moved to the trees in the yard.

On his last day of school, he got in a fight with several boys. He tried to impress them with his genitals, believing this would startle them. They beat him until he was bloody and had pissed himself. The school phoned Mr. K.: Thomas had been expelled but could return when he decided he wanted to be a boy again.

"It's not his fault," Mr. K. said. "He believes too much."

Mr. K. rarely saw the boy after the expulsion. When he did, the child was naked and alternated between walking upright and on all fours.

"What's happening to my spots?" the boy asked one afternoon. It was the first time Mr. K. had heard the boy speak in more than a month.

"You don't have spots."

"Mom has spots. I'm like her."

Thomas showed his father his arms and back. Mr. K.

removed his glasses and rubbed his eyes.

"Those are freckles, Thomas."

The boy stood there looking pensive. He gnawed his lip and scratched his forehead.

"You mean, I'm like you?"


One of the snow leopard cubs at the zoo became sick and died. It was the male. It had quit eating the week before and started retching up frothy pools of green liquid. The zookeepers had been unable to evaluate the cub in the lab because Mrs. K. guarded over him. They shot her with three or four tranquilizers, enough to topple an elephant, but they only succeeded in infuriating her. Whenever they came close she flecked menstrual blood and vomit at the nosy zookeepers. Late at night, she licked the cub's fur smooth.

The older girl cub mauled her brother in the night. Mrs. K. had fallen asleep and the female cub split open her brother's neck. When the mother awoke and found the lifeless body, the female cub made a strange purr that Mrs. K. understood was a kind of lullaby. She did her best to imitate the sound.

"What happened?" Mr. K. wanted to know. He was on the observatory deck watching the scene unfold. The zookeeper explained the mysterious illness. Then he sighed.

"These things happen."

The husband watched as his wife licked the fur of the dead cub.

On the other side of the enclosure was a group of young boys. They were huddled in a circle. They looked the same age as Thomas. One of the boys threw a rock. It bounced off Mrs. K.'s right hind leg. She skittered beneath the tree. Another rock came down. It hit her on the shoulder. Her eyes squinted, but she did not flinch. She shielded the cub's lifeless body from the barrage of falling rocks. Mr. K. found a rock of his own. He held it in his trembling hands.

Mr. K's first attempt to liberate the zoo was a failure. He leaped over the gate sometime past midnight but was discovered before he could even get to the monkey cages. He spent the night in jail. The next morning he promised a judge he would never do such a ridiculous thing again. He tried unsuccessfully to secure a court order to have his wife forcibly removed from the zoo.

"This is the twentieth century, Mr. K.," the judge said. "The prerogative of wives against the wishes of their husbands is of no concern for this court. Marriage is not an endangered species requiring government intervention."

The second attempt, one month later, was a success. He managed to free the foxes, gorillas, rhinos, and half the kangaroo population without difficulty. The other animals took some concerted effort. When the first zookeepers arrived the next morning the flamingos were strolling about, the lions preening on the grass, and the hippos ambling about in search of a new pond. Only the giraffes and meerkats were still in their enclosures.

Mr. K. felt he had no choice but to stage an escape. For months he had tried to convince his wife to leave the zoo. She had been unresponsive to his attempts at intimacy which the zookeepers suggested might be the only way to woo her back to civilization. He had waited until late February—the peak of snow leopard mating season, according to the book he borrowed from his son—but she was altogether uninterested in his efforts. She did not seem to recognize the songs they once listened to together on the antique record player, the flowers he brought made her sneeze, and she shat on the picnic dinner he prepared.

He discovered that in fourteen years of marriage he had forgotten how to flirt and the best he could muster were awkward smiles, bad jokes, and uncomfortable silences. He called her Lulu, his favorite pet name for her. He tried to jar her memory with simple remembrances. He reminded her of the time she slipped at the restaurant and broke two fingers. Or when her high-heel was caught in the sewage grate in the middle of the road and he directed traffic for half an hour because she wouldn't leave behind her favorite shoes. During the long stretches when he would talk, she perched on all fours beneath the tree with the girl cub and listened, almost as if she was trying to forget.

When Mr. K. lowered the ladder into the enclosure during that midnight raid, he thought he would have her out in a few minutes. He called her name in a whisper, then shouted. When she leapt down from the tree he almost did not recognize her. She was remarkably clean and her hair, while longer, was neatly pinned in a bun. She looked taller, even though she remained in a perpetual crouch. It was dark but her eyes were a striking green, aching with confidence.

What attracted her was not his voice but the ladder. She sniffed it, eyeing him as if she sensed the deceit. She licked herself. He called her name again and she yawned.

When Mr. K. started to climb down the ladder she hissed. He tried to take her hand and she flecked menstrual blood at him.

They rounded up most of the escaped animals. Some had been shot by local hunters, others euthanized, the rest sent to live on bio-reserves. Some were never seen again. The zoo closed down for violation of city ordinances. Mrs. K. was one of the last animals removed. They gave her a fresh change of clothes and sat her on the bench while they retrieved her husband. Mr. K. came along shortly looking every bit a man defeated. For the previous two weeks he had locked himself in the sea turtle exhibit trying to be closer to his wife, but nobody mistook him for anything other than a damn fool.

They walked slowly into the empty parking lot. Pleasant weather ruled the skies. Mr. K. talked about putting new locks on the doors. After showering, they ate. The children were asleep. The house suddenly seemed foreign to them both.

Undressing in the dark, Mrs. K. stumbled over a box of old photographs. Her husband must have retrieved them from the attic. Dimming the light, she studied them, glancing over her shoulder to make sure her husband was still asleep.

They were boring photos. Weddings. Birthdays. Her husband had no eye for capturing the moment. Suddenly, halfway through the stack, she recognized her younger self smiling on an old cobblestone bridge. Somewhere in the Austrian Tyrol, if she wasn't mistaken. The photograph was taken the day before she jumped off that bridge. It happened decades ago, the first time she was away from home, the first time on her own. She had left everything behind, crossed the vast ocean alone, and hitchhiked from town to town. Ate cheese. Breathed deeply that foreigner's air buzzing with starlight. She took a job in a bakery. Flour, water, and salt. That was her religion. Before sunrise she kneaded dough, baked it and sold it to people whose words she did not understand. In the evening she strolled by the river, astonished by its current. It seemed so fragile. Nothing daring to disturb its solitude. Without thinking, she wanted it. Perhaps the first time she wanted anything in her young life.

She jumped early in the morning. This was a Tuesday, the best day for a woman to leap from a bridge, according to the library. An old bridge, maybe hundreds of years. Laid stone by stone for men to cross and women to leap. How many jumpers had it known? Was she one of a thousand? Or something more special? She convinced herself only the fall would tell her. Yet the fall was too brief to even startle her, only enough to help her feel what it was like to be close to the edge of elsewhere.

Nobody rescued her. A man letting his dog piss in the river smoked his cigarette as she swam to the muddy bank and collapsed out of breath.

A few hours after leaping off the bridge, she discovered the cut on her thigh. She stared at it, disappointed to the point of betrayal, because already the wound was beginning to scab. For a time she peeled away the crusts to look at the wound. Then it scarred. Not long after she left the town for another and met Mr. K. on a Wednesday, the best day to fall in love, he later convinced her.

Lying in bed, Mrs. K. reached for the rubbery scar. Where was it? Her hands groped awkwardly. Maybe she had remembered this all wrong. Maybe there was no leap. No scar. No, it was there, only faint. So very faint. It had—for a day, maybe less?—been a magnificently discolored thing, but now, surrounded by charcoal shadows creeping over the walls, Mrs. K. felt only its absence. The wonder of this astonished her softly. Like stepping into the lobby of the hotel where dreams are made and finding all the rooms occupied. Without knowing why she longed for that moment after jumping off the bridge, that moment when her face broke through the water's surface, eyes opened, so relieved by the fatal lack of color.

# The Good Nazi Karl Schmidt

Over the holiday break we got a pet Nazi. This was a little un-expected. My mother says it is not really a pet. She's very par-ticular that, beneath the costume, the Nazi is in fact a man, a very sad and troubled man who needs our love and sympathy and forgiveness, and under no circumstances should we tell the other children or their parents we have a pet, especially not a pet Nazi. I'm not sure I believe her. The Nazi answers when I call him, is waiting for me when I come home from school, watches me fall asleep, and eats whatever I feed him. That sounds like a pet to me.

The Nazi is in fact Mr. Karl Schmidt. He's lived in town fifty-three years. Before being a Nazi he was a German. Not too long ago I brought the Nazi in for Show-and-Tell. All the children straightened in their seats to get a better view of the Nazi at the front of the class. It is easy not to notice Mr. Karl in a crowd. His hair is silver and his face plain, a little pinkish around the cheeks. He could be anybody's grandfather. That day he wore a tweed jacket. His pants were finely ironed and pleated down the front.

Mr. Karl did not say much about the war. He worked as a pastry chef in one of the camps. Nazis, he said, had vora-cious sweet tooths. If the Allies had bombed the sugar fac-tories, he said, the war would have ended much sooner. He held out his hands. Everyone smacked their lips as they got to touch the Nazi's hands.

Mr. Karl explained how after the war he tried to have himself punished. He dressed in his full SS uniform and waited at his house for the Allies to kick down the door. Nothing happened. He surrendered at the courthouse. They searched the archives. Karl Schmidt was not on the register of crimes against humanity. The lawyers questioned him. Mr. Karl confessed he was a monster. He wept. No, the lawyers told him. You don't act like a Nazi. You must have been one of the good ones. The magistrate dismissed his case. They declared him a reformed Nazi.

The other children were restless. They paid attention in social studies. They knew about Nazis. They wanted details. When you dream of the dead are they naked or clothed? What do Nazis eat for breakfast? Do bodies make noises after they're dead? Did you make a necklace from Jew teeth? Mr. Karl could not answer any of these questions. Someone said maybe Mr. Karl was not a real Nazi. Someone else said he was just pretending. Mr. Karl said, We cannot pretend to be what we already are.

Mr. Karl shuffled awkwardly on the playground, his chin pressed to his chest, his mouth twisted. He sat on the bench and watched the children play.

Look at his sneakers! someone joked. Would a Nazi actually wear sneakers rather than loafers? Mr. Karl sat there, staring at his sneakers until someone threw the kickball at his face.

I received an A- for my Show-and-Tell report. Ms. Stanley wrote one comment in red ink: QUESTIONABLE HISTORY. This led to the incident and why I am now in detention. I am supposed to be writing what I have learned from the incident and why pretending is inappropriate, but when you put a boy like me in detention with a ream of paper you're asking for trouble.

I am not a troublemaker. My father says it is not every day a fifth-grader like me leapfrogs into the seventh grade and I am at the age when one must learn about the bread and butter of history and not that liberal feel-good shit on the news. I know about Nazis. My father once showed me a pair of socks he keeps wrapped in tissue paper. These were special socks. Project Angora, he said. That's when the Nazis made socks from the fur of genetically-modified rabbits for pilots and U-boat captains. I touched the socks. They were very soft. I brought the socks to class. I could shoot torpedoes at an enemy ship if I was wearing socks like these. I told Ms. Stanley it's easy to kill people when you're comfortable *and* at a distance. She started to say something then stopped and here I am in detention. It is an odd thing to be a child. It is even stranger to be an adult and not know how to finish a sentence.

I'm getting ahead of myself. I'm in detention because of what happened with my pet Nazi.

News of a Nazi at the seventh grade Show-and-Tell gets around. Mr. Karl and his wife were invited to dinner parties. Nobody in town had ever seen a reformed Nazi. Others were not so enthused. One morning Mr. Karl went to fetch the newspaper and found a mangled rabbit carcass on his lawn. Someone had written in blood on the door: BUTCHER. One afternoon a rock came through the window with a note wrapped to it with a rubber band: GO HOME, NAZI SCUM.

Mr. Karl met with the local rabbi and explained he wanted to make restitution for his crimes and wondered if an apology would end the animal butchery on his lawn. The rabbi told Mr. Karl Jews have been wondering that same thing for five thousand years.

Not many people showed up at the synagogue for Mr. Karl's official apology. Most were old like Mr. Karl and wore etherized expressions. Mr. Karl talked for hours. He apologized.

He confessed guilt. Mr. Karl told them he could no longer pretend this never happened. He held up his hands and told them these were the hands of a poor soap-maker, not a butcher. Nobody was interested in Mr. Karl's remorse. They appreciated his shame and expressed admiration for the eloquence of his guilt, but after fifty-three years it was time to move forward. Let the dead make sense of the dead, the rabbi told Mr. Karl.

It was all too much for Mr. Karl's wife. She left him. She had not known about the good Nazi Karl Schmidt. She had only known Karl who worked forty-two years at the R&R Soap Factory. Karl who kept his lawn neatly trimmed. Karl who sang Christmas carols. Mr. Karl who loved Christmas. Nazis are very enthusiastic about decorations, you know.

It was my mother's idea to have Mr. Karl come live with us. Every week we go to the pet shelter and rescue an animal. That's my mother's gift—she finds homes for strays. We were at the shelter wandering the back rooms when who should we see inside one of the kennels but Mr. Karl Schmidt. My mother wanted to know how a man ended up in an animal cage but the people at the shelter shrugged and said there were too many strays to keep track of.

Mr. Karl had let himself go. He sat in the corner in his own feces stroking a maniacal beard and polishing the medals on his old SS uniform. Detention is cruel and ridiculous, but it's not easy being a reformed Nazi.

So we rescued Mr. Karl.

Before leaving the shelter he had a consultation with the veterinarian. My mother said it was ridiculous but this was the policy for strays.

Mr. Karl refused to take off the uniform. The Nazi hunters will be looking for me, he said, slumping against the wall, weary and frustrated with a shame nobody else wanted to acknowledge. He insisted his name was on *the list*.

Mr. Karl had seen a program on the television about the men and women dedicated to searching out and punishing former Nazis. Like this one episode, where a ninety-five-year-old blind grandfather was extradited from Singapore. The Nazi hunters had testimony from witnesses claiming the grandfather had been a butler to a commander at the labor camp in Frohburg which may or may not have made the grandfather an accessory to the murder of a gypsy. During his trial for crimes against humanity, the grandfather was only allowed to wear his pajamas. Then he died in his sleep in a prison cell and everyone said they were glad the monster was dead.

This is all true. Believe me, you can't make up history.

The veterinarian checked Mr. Karl's heart rate and listened to him breathe. Turns out Mr. Karl did not have fleas. When the veterinarian suggested we find a clinic that specialized in psychological disorders, Mr. Karl tapped the center of his chest and said the pain was here. No, the veterinarian corrected, tapping the side of Mr. Karl's head: all pain is *here*.

My father was not pleased with our new pet. After a few weeks I asked him why Karl wanted to be a Nazi so bad and he said it was no different than me and baseball. Last year I tried out for the baseball team. I practiced every day. I wanted to be a baseball player more than anything. After tryouts the coach told me I can't hit, can't throw, and round the bases like a fruit fly that has lost one of its wings. My father said we're all really good trying to be the thing we are not, but we're miserable at being what we are.

This explains why Mr. Karl decided to become a Jew. Oh, yes. This really happened. Let me explain.

Mr. Karl slept on the floor in my room. He was my pet, after all. He stayed up late worrying about the Nazi hunters. What if they don't find me? What if they don't recognize me? What if they've forgotten about me after all these years?

I told Mr. Karl maybe he should look to God for his answers. I don't know much about religion but I've heard my father say more than once that people who believe in God may be miserable but at least they're being miserable with a purpose. That's what Mr. Karl needed—a purpose for his misery. There are too many religions, Mr. Karl said. Not a problem, I said. I told Mr. Karl he should become a Jew. I had given a report last year on the five-thousand-year history of the Jews and they are the religion to beat. Mr. Karl said it was sweet of me to be so encouraging but there was probably a quota for the number of Jews at any time. Besides, he said, what about the Nazi hunters? How will they find me if I become a Jew? It took me a few days to think about that. Then I came up with the answer: when the Nazi hunters put his name on *the list* all those years ago they must have known that someday he would become a Jew. I told him they're not looking for Karl Schmidt, but Kalev Schmeichel.

We agreed this was only logical.

The next morning at breakfast we announced to my father that Karl the Nazi would become Kalev the Jew.

My mother dropped the eggs. My father chewed his toast and pushed his spoon around in the oatmeal. Then he shrugged, resigned to this new development in human evolution. He said that if God can make pomegranates grow in the desert then it's possible to turn old Nazis into Jews.

Mr. Karl went to synagogue like a zealot and pretty soon it was time for his circumcision ceremony. The rabbi explained to Mr. Karl and Mr. Karl explained it to me.

It was a sacred event. This is how HaShem gathers his elect. The rabbi quoted the prophets who taught to remove the foreskins of thy heart and let thy flesh be not a stranger to mine eye. He told Mr. Karl that which is shameful must be circumcised and so long as he had that unseemly thing between his legs he would forever be a Nazi. It is written, the rabbi told him, that one cannot be cleansed if he is not first soiled. How can God heal us if he first does not make us bleed? Well, Mr. Karl had a few concerns. He was concerned about a God who requires men to drop their pants to get into heaven. He said that if God wants to look at his cock he has to pay for that privilege like anybody else.

I apologize for using inappropriate language, but Ms. Stanley always criticizes us when our themes are not authentic.

I knew all about circumcision. I got an A+ on my World Religions report. I told Mr. Karl what really happens with a circumcision. You see, when Abraham was circumcised all those years ago a weird thing happened. On the eighth day the foreskin grew back. So, Abraham had it removed a second time. Every eighth day until the harvest moon Abraham removed his foreskin only to see it magically return. Mr. Karl wondered what God could possibly want with so much foreskin. That's simple. I told him it was for the Messiah. You see, after each circumcision the rabbi speaks a few magic words, then once it's finished he sends the foreskin with a courier to Jerusalem where it's carefully stored in a vault with all the other Jewish foreskins across the globe. It's been that way since the beginning of the Jews. At the appointed hour, a council of rabbis will fashion the millions of foreskins into the Messiah who will then drown the world with his piss and leave behind only the sanctified. This is all in the Midrash, by the way. Look it up. Well, except the last part. I made that up. But I told Karl everything else was true. Mr. Karl said my story was disgusting. I told him it was just good religion.

The circumcision took place at our house. There was a nice turnout. People arrived early, eager to find a good seat.

The men formed a circle around Mr. Karl. The rabbi whispered a prayer. Mr. Karl glanced around the room. Many of our friends and neighbors had come out of curiosity. Their faces were nice and they were nasty. When the rabbi said *amen* the other Jews said *amen* and a few of the neighbors made the sign of the cross.

It was time to remove the SS uniform. The knife steadied in the rabbi's hand. Mr. Karl struggled, suddenly unsure what was happening. He shouted they were hurting him. Someone in the crowd yelled to take off the uniform. Mr. Karl was begging for them to stop. They pushed me out of the way. I screamed for the men to stop. I screamed they were hurting my pet. Nobody listened. The rabbi started mumbling another prayer. He looked possessed.

In a few minutes the circumcision had become a dismemberment. There were scraps of Nazi uniform and medals scattered all over the carpet. There were fluffy angora socks. The rabbi sorted through the pieces but nobody saw Mr. Karl. Someone pointed out the window and said there was a naked man hiding in the bushes. When we looked we found nobody.

People nibbled on crackers. They spoke in hushed voices. Someone said it was a pity because Mr. Karl would have made a nice Jew. Someone else said he was an impostor. The rabbi said that since the days of Abraham the birth of a Jew has been a mess and a mystery.

When I shared all this for my theme on WHAT DID YOU DO OVER THE HOLIDAY BREAK? there was an incident. I don't want to talk about it. It wasn't pretending, and even if it was it wouldn't be inappropriate. I got a pet Nazi. I lost my pet Nazi. These things happened. I cried. Of course I cried. I wanted to go look for Mr. Karl who would be cold and hungry and might not know the way home. I wanted to be with my friend who was now just another stray. My parents wouldn't let me. They said I should stop reading so much history and stick to science where things make sense.

# A Genealogical Approach to My Father's Ass

Olaf Haber, respected oat farmer, ate raw human buttocks in the closing days of the third Silesian War. He never fired his weapon in combat. He never saw the ocean. He never met his son. It is written he was an accomplished kisser. His grandson, Heinrich Haber, suffered a case of debilitating hemorrhoids in his twenty-second year. Unable to sleep in his condition one night, he wandered the streets of Ansbach where he shortly found himself in a tree angling his bare bottom to the moon as instructed in one of Goethe's poems, convinced the moonlight would alleviate his discomfort. He was shot in the left buttock by the town's Bürgermeister, on whose property Heinrich was trespassing. This relieved the pain of the hemorrhoids but not the heart as the musket ball was removed with the help of the Bürgermeister's daughter who fell in love with young Heinrich. In Ansbach, it is a local tradition even today that when the Bürgermeister's daughter gets engaged her fiancé must be shot in the ass. Their grandson, Karl Wilhelm Habermeyer, became a Lutheran minister in America. Those of his congregation could attest that when the reverend Habermeyer spoke with the power of the Holy Spirit you felt it tingling in your sphincter. Karl Wilhelm attributed his gift to the physical abuse he endured as a young man when his father would swat his backside with the family Bible. My grandfather, John Gilbert Habermeyer, designed the gluteal cushions for astronauts on the Apollo 8 mission. It was his heart, not his ass, which gave out in the end. Yesterday, I felt my father's ass. I was helping him use the toilet. He no longer remembered how. The neurons in his head, weary from genealogy, had fizzled into a gray haze. He wrapped his arms around my neck like a baby baboon while I wiped. It did not feel the way I imagined. It did not feel like the ass that held up the belt he slammed against the bathroom door after I called him Jabba the Hutt. Or the ass that produced blue darts around Boy Scout campfires. Or even the ass that fidgeted nervously on the hospital chair as he held me the night my asthma wouldn't let me breathe. It felt cold and limp and alien, heavy with the science of lost futures.

## Your Tragedy Is Important to Us

Nine months after the accident the fire department rented out the school gymnasium and put on display the artifacts recovered from the wreckage. For weeks they had been mailing items to the families of the victims. So many items had gone unclaimed the fire chief decided to sponsor an event to regain public trust.

We had mistakenly received a sweater in the mail. It came in a plastic bag. It was red with two oblong holes. It could have belonged to a boy or a girl. I stretched it on the floor and tried to imagine the body that would fit inside. I had difficulty picturing the child's smile. I could imagine the face, only there was never a mouth, like it had been swept away by the flames after the school bus tumbled down the ravine.

We mailed the sweater back to the fire department but three days later it was redelivered. The mailman said he was just doing his job and I should lodge a formal complaint with the city. I told him I didn't mind. Sometimes the best way to deal with tragedy is to press right up against it.

My husband watched me fold the sweater with the rest of the laundry. He reread the invitation letter to the event signed by the fire chief.

YOUR TRAGEDY IS IMPORTANT TO US, it said.

"We don't have any children," my husband said with a calm disbelief.

He tried to put his arms around me, trembling like he did when he got upset.

Several parents arrived unprepared. Two fathers wrestled on the floor over a lunchbox and had to be removed. Mostly, people were quiet and paced the aisles as if they were in a museum.

At the door they handed out raffle tickets. It was possible, the fire chief told us, that some parents wouldn't recover anything, so unclaimed items would be raffled.

"That's sick," said my husband.

"It's better than nothing," I told him.

I rummaged through blankets and teddy bears, sneakers and backpacks and half-melted crayons. I looked for something familiar. I found the sweater. I folded it neatly, then stuffed it under a heap of clothes.

When the time came we did not win the red sweater in the raffle.

In the parking lot my husband sat on the hood of the car and pretended to burn his hand with a cigarette while some children watched, believing it was the coolest magic trick they had ever seen.

I followed the couple who had claimed the sweater. I awkwardly confessed what had happened: watching the story develop on the news, the sleepless nights, how we had been sent the sweater by mistake. I apologized for washing off the smell of burnt asphalt and smoke.

"It's a nice sweater," I said.

I asked if I could see a picture of their child. It would help me find some closure.

"There must be a mistake. We're not parents," the husband said. His wife clutched the sweater against her chest.

"Someday," she said, "we want a child of our own."

The couple got in their car. I pressed my hand against

the window—maybe I wanted to stop them, maybe I just wanted to feel something, I don't know—but then my husband pulled me away. He said to keep walking. He said not to turn around.

His hands were warm. I could feel where the cigarette had pretended to burn his palm. Days later, if I concentrated enough, I could still feel that burn, and for once it felt so good.

## The Fertile Yellow

"We're getting pregnant tonight," my wife says.

I am up on the roof where the last thing I do every Thursday evening as the sun goes down is squeeze fifty pounds of grapefruit juice over shingles and rain gutters and down the chimney. It is a ceremony. After half a day at the office crunching the numbers, still in a daze from the morning whirlwind my wife calls making love but is more like animal acrobatics that belong on the nature channel, I pick up the weekly crate of grapefruit we get wholesale from Red Dahlquist, swing by General Lee's to listen to The Electric Prunes on the jukebox while I sip a whiskey sour, then storm through the door of the house where my wife gives me a precoital kiss that always tastes like red wine and I change clothes before heading into the garage to get the ladder, and then into the yard where I haul the crate of grapefruit onto the roof and start squeezing like a man possessed. And every Thursday as the sun goes down my wife pokes her head out of an upstairs window and reminds me: We're getting pregnant tonight. Ten o'clock. Don't forget.

I lie on the gablet roof of a house that has been in my family three generations and suck a grapefruit to the rind as I take in a view of the sky. I'm familiar with this picture. Soon, ten o'clock will come and go and before long the sun rises for the whole experiment to begin one more time.

My hands are cramped from squeezing too much grape-fruit so I come inside to soak them in a bowl of hot water. My wife is washing dishes and she reminds me again: We're getting pregnant tonight. Ten o'clock. Don't forget.

"I've already started the grapefruit," I say, holding up my hands as evidence.

"No, grapefruit is on Thursdays," my wife says without looking at me. I can sense the resentment in her voice. "To-day is Friday. Friday is eggs. Don't mess this up, Jack. I swear to God, don't mess this up for me tonight."

I sit there confused, staring at my hands. "Wait, today is Friday?"

My wife takes advantage of this moment to call her sister into the room. Ann came to live with us once we got rid of the cat. This was near the beginning of the conception mania when my wife read an article about litter and toxoplasmosis and saw photographs of thalidomide babies with fingers that looked like chopped carrots. That was the end of the cat.

Ann is a kind of perfectly human but surrogate pet. She is seven months pregnant and round as the moon. When we first found out, my wife was ecstatic. We had Ann on twenty-four hour surveillance. I took notes: how many steps she took each day, the shape of her bowel movements, what television shows she watched, the decibel level of her laugh, and what flavor of gum she chewed. My wife was convinced Ann's pregnancy was an information system that would un-lock the secrets to her own uterus. We no longer discuss it.

The two of them empty a fat, manila envelope and con-sult the ovulation charts and compare them with the annota-tions on the fertility calendar. There are graphs of ovulation phases and grids to track daily body temperature, coital as-sessments, and levels of cervical fluid. Our marriage has been reduced to a series of colored grids, bubbles, and bell curves.

"You lose, Jack," my sister-in-law smiles. "It says clearly right here: Fridays are reserved for eggs."

I rub the sides of my head. "I thought we agreed to stop wearing underwear on Fridays?"

My wife leans back in her chair with a disgusted look on her face. This is a love trial, she calls it. Bringing life into this world is all about love, but sometimes that love has to hurt. She looks like she might cry. She lights a cigarette. As part of our agreement she gets one every day and I do not complain about the fertility exercises. Ann is not pleased and stands on the other side of the kitchen, wafting away smoke while complaining that if her baby is born sickly then it is my fault.

"If this baby pushes its way out of my vagina and they find out it's retarded then I'm going to blame *you*, Jack. This baby isn't going to live in my womb for nine months, Jack, then come out my vagina, *my* vagina, Jack, and be retarded because you can't control your wife."

She blows a kiss towards me. I pretend to dodge out of the way and gaze out the window where the kiss might have floated away. She laughs. I wink.

"She's your sister," I say.

"You two have no consideration for my vagina," Ann says.

Ann likes the word vagina. She is obsessed. Her vagina must not be excluded from any civilized conversation. She uses the word freely as a noun or adjective, and even a verb. My vagina dilates ten centimeters at delivery. I vaginaed to the store. Have you ever vaginaed like that before? What a vagina day, don't you think? What the hell are they thinking, that stupid vagina vagina? It aches. It's sore. It burns. My vagina's lonely and talks to me at night. My vagina doesn't have a father. On more than one occasion I've glanced casually under the table during dinner to make sure she is not sneaking her vagina any scraps.

"Maybe we should mix it up tonight," I say, turning to look at my wife and not wanting to entertain for the moment the love/hate relationship I have with Ann. "Get out of the routine? Just a glass of wine and some good music. Maybe slow dance naked in the rain. Wasn't that in the book?"

When we got serious about making babies we went to the library and looked for a book about conception. The librarian recommended some bestsellers on pop psychology but my wife wanted to go old school. She went through special collections until finding Cunningham's *A Brief Chronicle of Human Fertilization Vol. I.* He was a student of Lazzaro Spallanzani. The book was published in 1843. It is four inches thick. We read the damn thing cover to cover, every line of pseudo-scientific bullshit.

"I just want the goddamn eggs, Jack," my wife says with a no-nonsense voice.

"Okay, so we get eggs," I say. "How many eggs do you want?"

"However many it takes," she says, but I know we're not talking about the same eggs anymore.

My wife knows better than most that you cannot make a baby without first scrambling some eggs. Somewhere in that manila envelope there is no doubt mention of our forty-four visits with eleven different gynecologists in three different states, to say nothing of the six meetings with an unlicensed pregnancy specialist and the fourteen visits to the fertility clinic, including the time we had a coital performance review by a three-panel medical board. There is certainly a file on her four miscarriages and the ill-effects of a sewn cervix. We are well acquainted with week nine during pregnancy because that is when the human heart finishes dividing and our babies have never made it past week nine because their hearts have too many holes. It's a family defect. Her gynecologist insists the data on her ovaries is positive. Her tubes are twisted the right way. Her womb has an exceptional twenty-eight degree tilt. My internist insists there is no such thing as an overly erect penis and some of my sperm might have three heads and no tails, but so does any man who listens to The Electric Prunes. My wife refuses drug therapies and will not grow a child in a petri dish. She insists we are not Dr. Frankenstein. I'm beginning to believe we are but have just learned to call ourselves by another name.

One day I came home for the usual 12:05 coital assessment and found my wife watching the home shopping network. There was a man, a genuine idiot, trying to sell mud from the Holy Land. He said his life changed years ago during a trip to Jerusalem when he had tried to drown himself. This was when he had no wife, no job, no hair, and suffered from constant urinary distress. So he rowed himself out into the middle of the Dead Sea and did his best Jesus impersonation. He made it three steps on the water before losing his balance.

"Best bath I ever took," he told us.

He had not bathed in six years. The host raved about the smell of the mud and salt in his hair. He had impregnated three different women and they all lived together on a ranch in southern Utah. Later, we read his story in the *North Star Gazette.*

"If you want to reach the impossible you have to attempt the absurd," he told the television camera.

The man was a fool, but foolishness is the salt that flavors a marriage.

Since then I have been delivered into mad bouts of pregnancy. On Mondays we take raw honey and aloe vera juice enemas. Tuesdays we eat an all-yogurt diet. Wednesdays we shampoo all our body hair with mail-order breast milk so our reproductive organs feel like they are in a safe environment. On Thursday I sprinkle grapefruit juice over the house to drive out unclean spirits. Fridays are a variety of eggs, minus the yolks which are bad luck. On Saturdays we wash the linens with coyote urine which helps increase sperm count. On Sundays we rest as the good Lord intended.

Not everything works. Lifting your legs like an acrobat after coital assessment is useless because sperm do not obey conventional laws of gravity. We've eaten carrots shaped like uncircumcised penises. My wife held her breath for two minutes after a coital assessment. I painted fertility symbols on my chest with fish guts. I howled at the sky and jumped up and down trying to alter the gravitational pull of the moon hoping it would tilt my wife's uterus back into place. We mastered the Weeping Willow position. We even applied a homemade balm from equal parts turmeric and garlic. At first we thought we were doing it wrong because nothing was happening and the book promised I would feel something. So, we sautéed the garlic and turmeric and mashed it into a fine paste, then my wife rubbed it all up and down the shaft. I felt it then. I wouldn't recommend it. Especially because I didn't get a blowjob for a month.

We are still awaiting our answer from the gods. Any gods are welcome.

The grocery store is full of eggs. It's almost midnight. My wife was expecting me home hours ago but I kept driving down one road until I came to another and then followed the streets in an endless loop. All the streets looked like vaginas to me and all the lampposts like penises. I can't understand why we build our cities to look like reproductive organs, unless it means it is the great illness of our time. Even the stars are conspiring against me tonight and look like a thousand ova floating past each other in elliptical orbits, so close but always out of reach. That's all it takes, according to the book. One touch from a single sperm and a crust forms around the ovum to prevent a double fertilization. The sperm slips inside and the cellular bomb goes off. My wife and I have spent the last three years of our lives so close to each other her skin feels like my skin and there is barely room to breathe but our molecules have no chemistry.

Inside the store there are plenty of options for eggs. White or brown. Farm-raised or hormone free. There are jumbo, extra-large, large, even peewee-sized eggs. Want variety? Try eggs from chickens, quail, snake, duck, goose, pheasant, even emu. This doesn't begin to cover how to cook them: fried, poached, scrambled, boiled, pickled, deviled— the possibilities are endless.

There is a woman at the other end of the refrigerated aisle looking for eggs. She opens and closes the cartons inspecting them. Sitting in her cart is a young boy in pajamas. The kid can't be much older than two. He looks miserable, like he cannot believe he's been taken out of his crib for this nonsense.

"Shouldn't that baby be asleep?"

The mother gives me a nasty look and I realize I've been speaking out loud without knowing it. "You wouldn't understand," the mother says, continuing her search for the holy grail of eggs. "You must not be a parent."

I'm a patient man. Any husband trying to impregnate his wife must be. But I hate this woman. Not because she deserves it, but because she can no longer conceive of a time without her child. Her existence is absolute because she exists in relation to another. She is a mother. That leaves an indelible scar all the way down onto the genetic code. Me? My mother died ten years ago. I never knew my father. Those wounds have healed. I am nobody's son. The closest thing I've fathered is a fetus the size of a grape with a heart full of holes.

I drop one of the eggs on the floor. It shatters. The boy giggles.

I crack another two dozen, quickly, until there is a nice thick layer of yolk. The shells crunch under my feet as I do a little dance. The mother takes a step toward me. I don't hesitate. I wind up like Sandy-fucking-Koufax and hurl that goddamn egg right for her oversized noggin. It sails right past her and smashes into the kid's face. I hear the kid scream, but everything is happening in slow motion so I watch the egg explode—the shell and yolk and whites suspended in the air.

The mother keeps screaming and I can't understand why until I realize it's not because I threw the egg. She's not screaming at me. She's screaming because that was no normal egg. A puddle of yolk expands on the floor. At first it was just a little trickle but now it flows down the aisle. The more it travels the faster it expands.

People run out of the store. They shut the doors and windows behind them trying to keep the yolk contained. I'm trapped. The yolk is rising. I know I am not dreaming because only the ridiculous can feel this real.

In a matter of minutes the entire store is a pool of yolk and I'm struggling to keep afloat. Then I stop trying to resist. I go limp. I remove my clothes. I sink inside the yolk. It fills my ears and the insides of my nose. I breathe it. It's warm. Then I understand what Cunningham wrote in his *Chronicle of Human Fertilization*: "The life of a mammalian sperm is a dull, pointless exercise whose singular outcome is death. Even the sperm that fertilizes commits a kind of suicide once inside the ovum. To be a sperm is not about finding existential closure but learning to ride the ejaculatory wave."

Outside the store people have come close to the windows to watch me swim. I alternate between butterfly and the breast strokes. I must look something like a bizarre merman in a primal, Freudian scene. The yolk fills to the ceiling and the pressure intensifies. My ears ring, so deep it upsets the beating of my heart. The glass windows crack and eventually shatter. The yolk spills like a tidal wave into the street and I glide on the waves, lunging in a sea of fertile yellow.

I open the door to the house with a carton of eggs and a pink citation slip from the sheriff who was kind enough to drive me home. There is a crusty glaze of dried yolk on my hair and skin.

Ann pretends to be asleep on the sofa. I pull the blanket over her and kiss her forehead. My hand drifts down her neck until it settles on her belly that is round like the moon. It would be so much easier if she had actually swallowed the moon. I feel the baby turning. He must be like his father, the prisoner of some strange aquatic acrobatics. Ann looks at me with a half-smile, her hand over mine pressing down and the baby's hand on the inside pressing out, and for a moment I feel like the equals sign in a balanced chemical equation.

Before I can get under the blanket with her Ann pushes me away gently.

"Not tonight," she says. "She needs you. Go to her."

My wife waits for me under the sheets. She works on her breathing rhythms. The lights are off. If we see each other the whole spell might be broken.

In the bathroom I crack the remaining eggs into the sink, careful to separate the yolks from the whites. Dabbing a finger, I draw fertility symbols over my chest. I take a handful of kosher salt and sprinkle that over my skin and in my hair until it forms a nice crust. I look ridiculous. Nobody believes this is the way their life will turn out. This isn't in the handbook. Nobody tells you you'll be a thirty-something standing in front of a mirror bathed in yolk and crusted in sea salt looking like a grotesque spermatozoon. Nobody tells you how to hug a naked wife who can't get pregnant. Nobody tells you how to keep a marriage going when you're both empty vessels with so much dead-end love. Nobody tells you how to come to terms with being what you are. Nobody changes. Nobody evolves. We are tiny little molecules swimming in a vast cosmos, bumping into each other, shedding energy, gaining entropy, trying to replicate our own misfortune. From blastocyst to the grave this is what we are. We are what we are.

But for now I forget all that. I do my stretches. I stretch my arms and legs far apart until I look like an X or a man condemned to a medieval torture wheel. I do this more than a dozen times. My wife read in one of the books that sperm assume the shape of their hosts and since she wants a girl whose hair she can braid I had better adjust my posture into an X as often as possible because she does not want little boys that look like me.

When I'm ready I go to her. I curl into her body, the two of us assuming the cross-eyed Margaret position. When I open my mouth to tell her what I've done, to confess my betrayals, she fills it with kisses. She whispers in my ear the word for egg in fifteen different languages. I do not speak. I am an enormous spermatozoon and I have one objective for the next thirty minutes: self-annihilation. She attacks me with more kisses. My arms go numb. My legs are twisted around her and dangle off the side of the bed like the tail of some hideous creature. She licks the dried egg off my body. The salt flakes away. With each kiss I can feel myself getting heavier, my head bobbing side to side, and then it is as if I am being swallowed and falling down a long tunnel, and I cannot breathe—like there is a yolk wedged deep in the gallows of our throat.

## Veyo, Forgotten by the Mormons

We were in the tall grasses creeping on finches when we seen Mama run down the slope in her Sunday finest and throw herself in the creek trying to get to the other side. Papa stood there scratching at his hair like he was fixing a nest for a warbler. We thought she might have eaten some loco weed, or gone swimming near the pond where the government tested them bombs that made the llamas spit blood and the babies grow thirteen fingers. We were not surprised. Mama never cared much for Veyo.

Papa stood at the fence a good while watching her float downstream, then told us boys to wait inside the house and like good boys we said yes, father. Sometime later we seen the two of them walking up the path and Papa all smiles with an arm around her shoulder and Mama teetering one foot to the other, her eyes far off.

Later we lay in bed.

Mama's leaving, Brother said.

She left before.

Not like this.

Then he was quiet. That's what he did when his thoughts hurt him: shrug and get quiet and then head down to the creek.

We were always at the creek. Sometimes we fished, other times we just lay there in the mud, staring at that milky rib of moon.

I liked to come down in the grasses after we fried a mess of Sanpete trout and feel them mucking my insides, feeling heavy as they tried to put themselves back together. We listened for what the breeze said, but there was nothing, which is the sound of forgetting.

We been fishing since we been boys. Only creek in Veyo with splake the size of your leg. Freaks of nature. Papa told us the story. It was Mormons come south and use the waters for baptism. Never been the same since. The wrong end of a miracle. Once we reeled us a monster and after we cut her open and eaten a handful of eggs like Papa showed us we seen a little pocket watch tangled in her innards. It still counted the right seconds. After a miracle something is left behind, I suppose.

It took both me and Brother to carry her. It was beautiful.

We collected other heaps of fish in a hollowed out tree on the other side of the ridge. Spear em and watch em rot with their little mouths chewing on the air. You know, looking for other miracles. We didn't tell nobody about the heap. We had near a thousand fish and all of them rotted except the fish with the pocket watch inside her. We couldn't figure that one out. Why in god was she not rotted? Then Brother said she was so big and heavy she could not be carried up to god.

That was the most beautiful thought he ever had.

What's beautiful? Brother said, and then I realize I been talking out loud the whole time when I thought I was alone in my head.

Shut up, Brother.

Are you worried, Brother? Don't be, he said. Mama has nowhere to run.

He said he seen the maps and there is no way out of Veyo except on water. He used a piece of chalk to draw the maps on the floor. Then he showed me how the old Veyo creek went into Lake Panguitch and pretty soon you were floating in the Mfolozi outside of Mtubatuba.

One river is all rivers, Brother, he said.

So we can swim out of Veyo, I said. I had always wanted to leave Veyo. It is a big world I think. It would be pretty to see it all.

No, Brother, he said. You don't know how to swim.


At first we believed it would all go back to how it was. Just Mama and Papa and us boys. Then Papa fell down and broke his leg. When we came to see he was groaning like a sorry sack of bones and Mama at the top of the stairs like a mouse just escaped a trap, a kind of shame in her eyes but at the same time that look of agony we seen from her when she broke dishes when Papa was out in the fields and she thought nobody was looking.

There's been an accident, she said.

Papa wouldn't stand for no penny-grubbing doctor, so he waited at the bottom of them stairs to be raised by the lord. He said this family needed a miracle. He called on the lord for healing. Papa had once preached for the Mormons before us brothers were brothers, but then they ran out on the lord and Veyo. Not Papa. Stand ye in holy places. And so we have.

By supper we had all grown tired of his weeping and wailing prayers that didn't make it past the ceiling, so when he told me the lord did not descend for nobodies and perhaps needed some encouragement I went to the shed for the beadle mallet.

Thank *gawd*, Brother said, trying to hold back a laugh.

Papa told him not to blasphemy. Then he pressed my finger against the thigh of his good leg. The other one was busted up.

You aim it true, son, he said. God will see to the rest.

Yes, Papa, I said.

When I mashed the leg he twisted in his spittle with ears red as a turkey waddle and cursed the day of my birth.

It's a fair punishment, Mama said.

Do you think the lord will raise Papa? Brother wanted to know.

Only god will be the judge of that, Mama said.

In the end Papa raised himself off the stairs because the good lord was out to lunch or squatting over the other end of the earth so it could have rain, or something. Papa limped around the house leaving behind him a leaky mess. There was blood and pus and all kinds of drippings. Mama got her bucket of water and mopped it up, muttering something awful.

Then the men came and took Papa away. He had been lying on the stairs for days, like some old bear who lost his fur from too much scratching and now pretended not to have an itch. His leg was the size of a pumpkin, only a bit purply.

We watched from the trees as the men dragged Papa out of the house and put him in the car. Papa called them the devil's servants. He tried to run away. We threw some rocks at the men until Mama called us out of the trees. Then we watched them drive away to the sick house.

Has Papa been touched by the Holy Spirit? Is that why he can go away?

No, Mama said. He's just sick.

It sure looked like a spirit had a grip on him. That's the other miracle of Veyo. After the baptisms the Mormons called down the Holy Ghost out of heaven. It was supposed to just visit but the Mormons got greedy and took hold on that ghost and tore it up as many ways they could, some people even letting it get inside them, and other pieces just ignored like leftovers on a messy dinner plate.

Sometimes I been looking for a piece of that Holy Ghost. I hoped it would sweep me off my feet somewhere far far away. I creep out when Brother is asleep. Thought I saw it once or twice out in the alfalfa fields, but it wasn't the ghost I was looking for. That's the trouble with ghosts. It's always somewhere ahead or behind but never in front, always there when you're not looking and gone when you need it most. They are impolite things, ghosts are.

Mama got a bowl of vinegar and wiped the house clean. She cleaned doors and windows and stairs and ceilings and walls. All the places Papa left a stain. She wanted the house spotless. She wanted to erase what was.

She took us once to see him in the sick house. It was full of sick people. Who knew that with so much leftover Holy Ghost Veyo was such a sick place? The world is strange.

Papa said, I feel better.

Mama said, You are sick.

When we came back to the house she took out more vinegar and cleaned more furious than before until the house smelled like a brown headache.

That's when Brother said once she had the house clean there would be nobody to keep her from running.

Who's gonna save her from herself? Brother said. Papa's not here anymore.

That's when he decided it was up to us boys to watch over Mama. He told me what must be done. He said the family needed a miracle to stay together.

You're gonna kill her.

Nobody's killing anything, he said.

When I said we should just give her a hug, Brother said hugs are no good when you have a hole in your heart. All that squeezing just makes the hole bigger. Pretty soon you hug too much and you're just holding on to empty air.

Is that what you want? Brother said. You want Mama to be some ghost?

So we tried to keep Mama with us. We picked a mess of flowers that gave her sneezes and stuffed them under her pillow. She tossed them out the window.

Then Brother had the idea to spend all afternoon loosening the second porch step. She was always going down those steps in a hurry and Brother said she would fall and break her hip. But Mama never used the second porch step.

She did not drink the milk where we poured the lye. She never opened the closet at the end of the hall where we put the hornet nest, even after I had climbed the tree to fetch it.

At night I cried softly thinking about Mama not being there in the morning. What would we do without Mama to wipe the mud from our feet and the snot from our noses? What would happen if Mama was not there to hold our hands in church or lick our scrapes clean? Mama always said we were miracles, which is why she kept us inside her belly eleven months because when she was so heavy she had never before felt so close to god.

I asked Brother what would happen if Mama left and we weren't miracles. Without Mama, what were we?

Just boys, Brother. Just boys, he said.


Brother held down Mama's legs. He told me how to make the knots to rope her arms to the bedposts. She didn't fuss, like she knew it was coming.

Lie still, Mama, Brother said. It's just us boys.

Her eyes were open now and she could see the heap of fish we carried from the other side of the ridge. The big one had finally rotted, so it looked like we needed a different miracle. Perhaps the lord would provide.

As Mama watched us gather the fish she thought it was just another mess she would have to clean. She thought us brothers were there to throw fish slops all over the house. Then Brother told her he had figured it out. The heavy fish, us boys heavy inside her, father's leg heavy as a pumpkin. We had it all wrong before, Brother said, but now it made sense. When the lord wants something to move he makes it soft, like the air. When he wants it to stay put and not get swept away by the Holy Spirit he makes it heavy, like a fish.

Brother fisted the fish guts into his hand. He told Mama to open her mouth. Mama said no and Brother said yes.

Mama spit up the first slops with a yelp. She said it wasn't enough to make her heavy and Brother said God would be the judge of that. Brother had me hold her mouth open while he pressed fish inside her.

Good, Mama, Brother said. Good. We'll get through this together. Hold her hand, Brother.

After a while I asked if we were done.

No, Brother said. I think she's got other holes. He said it in a whisper.

Other holes?

We'll have to fill them too, Brother said.

We kept pressing fish inside her. It was almost morning. I asked if she was heavy yet.

Shut up, Brother, he said.

When our hands were sore from stuffing, Brother reached for the pocket watch. Mama was trembling now, like a mackinaw out of water. I held her hand. Her skin was slick like fish scales. I wanted the Holy Spirit to carry me far away from this place. But I had to see.

Don't worry, Mama, Brother said, winding up that old

pocket watch. He steadied his hand where she opened at the thighs.

It's nothing, Mama, Brother said. Just another miracle.

## An Unfinished Man

Six weeks after the funeral, the postal service continued to deliver mail for our neighbor's dead wife. The adults were dropping dead left and right. Mr. Landry had a heart attack in the teacher's lounge. Mrs. Rosamond took some pills for a headache and never woke up. Calvert Stevenson, who made funny faces whenever we walked past his yard, slipped off his roof. Mr. York was asking his wife a question when he choked on a cherry tomato. The neighbor's wife was not so different. One day she was with us, and then she was gone. We were kids. We paid attention.

Our parents took us to the funerals. We got fat on funeral potatoes and sparkling cider. We did our best to look depressed. When we ran out of tears, we had to fake our sadness like everybody else.

In our home there was always talk of the dead. My mother said the lake of fire and brimstone was not infinite. Some were doomed to be reborn as animals, others must wander as spirits to tempt the righteous, and those who had dishonored the image of God would cast off this human form and become the elements: the fornicators would be transformed into dirt and the liars blown hither and thither to serve as the wind. The world was a mysterious place carefully measured by the wisdom of God.

My father, the biologist, said this was nonsense and when

we were dead we became nitrogen, phosphorus, and methane. He showed me pictures of what it looked like in rabbits. Simple proteolysis, he said.

The mail was my comfort. The mail was the last routine in a neighborhood of chaos and spirits and unfinished questions. The mail was yeses and nos, black and white, inside and out. It carried on with or without us, indifferent to weather or public polls or the breadcrumb count in mother's meatloaf.

The neighbor and his dead wife, Brother and Sister Vance, were boring people and received boring mail. There were advertisements from Mr. Harvey who owned the used car lot. There were sympathy cards. Dead Sister Vance received a pen-pal letter from an orphaned child in Morocco, and Brother Vance received yet another notice from the library for an overdue book. Me and a few other boys stole the mail hoping it would offer a clue to the mystery of the dead adults. After reading the mail from the safety of the tree house, we rapped knuckles to see who had to return it to the appropriate mailbox.

One afternoon there was nothing but a padded manila envelope in Brother Vance's mailbox. When we opened it, there was a sudden breath of spoiled meat. We removed two sealed plastic packages. Lewis Snyder, who was the only one of us who paid attention in Biology, recognized they were kidneys.

"Whose kidneys?" we asked. "Sister Vance?"

They looked like oversized beans. They were knotted and wrinkled and diluted in a jellyish fluid. Were it not for the biohazard labels, they might have seemed perfectly at home in a grocery aisle.

Lewis said the kidneys must have been destined for some military laboratory with the rest of dead Sister Vance. He had read about it in an issue of *Weird Tales* he found in the attic. Jimmy Felch said he was lying. I said this must be a mistake or somebody's sick joke. Lewis shrugged. We all shrugged. We had read *Weird Tales*, too. We knew what was possible. But we didn't know whether to be horrified or enchanted, or if such feelings were distinct. We left the kidneys on Brother Vance's doorstep. We rang the doorbell. Then we hurried back into the tree house.

We used the telescope to watch Brother Vance through the window. He did not seem alarmed. He went to the cupboard for a bowl and filled it with ice. Then he placed the kidneys, still wrapped in the biohazard plastic, in the bowl. He sat at the kitchen table. He read the packaging label. His face was twisted with a half-smile, like he was trying not to scream. He turned the kidneys over in his hands. Occasionally, he glanced anxiously out the window as if hoping the mail truck would return.

That was last month.

My father sipped tea and tried not to grimace as he listened to Brother Vance tell this disturbing story. I listened from the stairs. Usually my mother sent me to my room when there were visitors, but she was in bed with a fever. I worried about why Brother Vance had come to us. Maybe he knew we took his mail. My father was neighborly with the old man, the two of them talking by the fence, and they often shook hands at church, but we had not been to church since before mother's first headache. Father said when God made up his mind to change things we would go back. Until then nobody inside these walls muttered so much as a God bless you.

Brother Vance told my father he had tried to return the kidneys to the hospital. He was greeted by a secretary who explained the hospital had a strict policy on organ donation. Brother Vance explained there had been a mistake and he was not donating them. He said he had signed paperwork. He told the secretary he wanted the matter resolved. Then he produced the kidneys in the glass mixing bowl full of ice and the secretary contacted her supervisor. The supervisor took one look at the kidneys and contacted the medical chief of staff. The two hospital men shuffled through papers. Eventually they apologized and admitted there had been a mistake. Brother Vance thanked God and told them how relieved he was his wife could be properly laid to rest. Except the hospital men refused. They said yes, there had been a terrible mistake, but there was nothing they could do.

The directory of the mortuary where Brother Vance's wife had been cremated also refused. He said he only performed services on complete bodies. It was a trade association policy. When Brother Vance asked if an exception could be made, the director showed him the Mortuary Services Manual, which clearly stated there was no fee scale for partial remains.

My father was already a little familiar with this sorry tale. Last month, right after we discovered the kidneys in the mail, Brother Vance had come seeking his scientific opinion. My father had examined the kidneys and insisted nothing could be done. The kidneys were dark and misshapen with yellowed cysts. I remember my father was concerned the kidneys might be a public health hazard, but Brother Vance had assured him he was not unstable or melodramatic. Just another desperate man in an impossible situation.

"Bodies are unpredictable," my father had told him. "Once I cut off a lizard's tail and it twitched for two months. Sometimes life holds on longer than it needs to."

Now Brother Vance had come back saying he had tried to take father's advice. He had tried to ignore the kidneys. He pulled the weeds from his lawn. He read books at the library. He changed the linens on the bed. He gifted his dead wife's clothes to the thrift shop. He let the color of the kidneys shift from burgundy to pale yellow with reddish patches. The undersides became brittle and hissed juices.

The smell was overwhelming. Unable to tolerate this heartache any longer, Brother Vance had buried the kidneys in his dead wife's garden.

"I've tried to forget," he told my father. "From my lips to God's ear, I tried."

My father had a difficult time understanding all this talk about the kidneys. He did not understand the problem. The wife was dead and the kidneys had been discarded. Was this a confession of grief? A plea for a blessing of comfort? Maybe he needed some money to pay the train fare to visit his daughter and take his mind off things? Brother Vance was the poorest man in the neighborhood. We were all poor, but Brother Vance was a fairy-tale beggar. Brother Vance insisted he was not interested in money. Finally, my father lost his patience.

"This is weird, Charles. Why are you telling me this?" he sighed, rubbing his bushy eyebrows so dramatically I actually thought they might fall off.

"I have a question," Brother Vance said in a low voice, almost ashamed. "Is it medically advisable for a man to eat his wife?" A sacramental quiet filled the room. I felt an ache in my bones. My father's face twisted.

"You're not making any sense," my father said, the blood rushing out of his cheeks. His hands trembled and he had to put down his tea.

"I am not ill," Brother Vance insisted. "I am no monster. The scriptures tell us that a man shall leave his parents and cleave unto his wife and none other and their flesh shall be as one. I am a poor, ignorant man. For years I believed when we die we become as the dust of the earth. I am a good believer, Brother Houseman. I put little faith in the mysteries of science. Then yesterday my wife returned from the dust in a way I did not imagine." He paused, licking his lips. "I buried her kidneys in the garden and now she has returned with the harvest. I have little money. There is little food in my cupboards except what I grow. So I ask you, Brother Houseman: Is it biologically sound for a man to consume his wife? Spiritually, it is permissible to twain our flesh as one, but what does science say?"

My father found it difficult to believe Brother Vance's wild imagination until the poor old man reached into his coat pocket and pushed into my father's hand a misshapen parsnip. It was from the garden. We had all seen one of Brother Vance's vegetables. He grew them every year. Sometimes he went door to door and other times our mothers sent us to his house with a little money and Brother Vance brought us into the root cellar and let us choose which vegetables we wanted.

What my father held was a parsnip but also not a parsnip. It was wet. It was ugly. It was fat and curved, unmistakably shaped like the dead wife's kidneys we found in the mail. Brother Vance insisted he had pulled a few dozen of these parsnips from his garden. He had searched for his dead wife's kidney where it had been buried, but now it was missing.

"Impossible," my father whispered. His hands trembled.

Brother Vance told my father that for the past month he had been a model of devotion with the parsnips, as if his wedding vows had been written for such an occasion. He kept them clean. They watched his wife's favorite television programs together. They prayed together. They did word puzzles. Sometimes they argued. When he feared moisture might accelerate their decay, Brother Vance sealed them in glass jars. On rare occasions he removed one of the parsnips from the jar and rubbed its skin. For a moment they were together again, Brother Vance said, just the two of them.

"We are much happier," Brother Vance smiled.

"Take me to see," my father said. I too wanted to see this Jack and the Beanstalk nightmare. Normally, my mother would have gone with my father, but she was still down with the fever. Father pointed to me on the stairs and told me to grab my coat.

Brother Vance led us into the root cellar. My father, suddenly second-guessing himself, ordered me to wait inside. He had no idea what was down there, and I was only a boy.

I waited in the kitchen. The floors were dirty and the windows smudged with grease. Empty cupboards. Rats whispered in their secret language behind the walls. It was a sad, lonely place to call a home.

"God have mercy on this house," my father whispered as he came through the back door. He stood in the doorway, his eyes far far away. Not even he had words for this mystery.

"Could it be the resurrection?" Brother Vance wanted to know.

"Not likely," my father told him. "If God is anything he is an artist, not a gardener."

My father said something must be done. He told me to tell the neighbors. As always, the neighbors were happy to witness a crisis and even more pleased to be part of such an unfortunate miracle. The women emptied their pantries and filled Brother Vance's cupboards with food so he did not have to eat the remains of his vegetable wife. Some of the men invited Brother Vance to talk with them. They were widowers. They sat in Brother Vance's kitchen and told stories of their dead wives with a well-oiled seriousness. One man cried. Another folded his arms philosophically across his chest. One of the men said he was unable to pack away his dead wife's clothes because it was the last smell of her in the house.

"Lady Death, thy perfume hath seduced me," the philosophical man said. "Goethe."

Another man said he still prepared a plate of food for his dead wife each night. Another had not washed his bed sheets in a month because the shape of his dead wife's head was on the pillow. A tall man with a voice like cigarettes said that since his wife died all the pictures of her in the photo album were out of focus. Nobody believed him, but he said it was true.

At one point the philosophical man leaned forward and told a riddle. "I am silent but full of screams, enormous but invisible. I crush a man but have no weight. I embrace all but have no body." He waited for the other widowers to take their guesses. Then, after a lengthy silence he said, "I am grief."

Late into the night they drank warm beer and continued this deranged mental autopsy. The women had all left, but the men continued to plant grief in each other's minds, a grief that swelled inside them like Jack's beanstalk.

Father told me pain was like that sometimes: pain made real by the ridiculous.

I wanted to stay but father told me there was nothing to see here and to go home. It was the first time I did not take his word as the law.

I used the side door and circled around the house. Then I lifted the doors and crept unnoticed into the root cellar. It was damp. There was frost on the windowpanes. A single light bulb dangled from the ceiling. I had trouble getting my feet to cooperate. I was caught between fear and the gruesome pleasures of anticipation. I stumbled through the root cellar. I wanted to look. I must know the salt from the sugar. I was filled with dread at seeing what was forbidden, but I would not be denied this nightmare.

I found the heavy glass jars on the shelf. There were dozens of parsnips. The jar hissed when I opened it. There was an odor. Maybe it was brimstone or maybe just nitrogen. Maybe it was something else. I held the parsnip under the light bulb. It ached with life and sent ripples in my chest. Sister Vance, or what was left of her, did not look ill. She was quiet and alone, but not the monster I had expected. It was just another of God's creations. Or his punishments. Or just somebody else's unfinished business.

I walked home in a daze, tripping over my feet. The night was ruined.

We heard nothing of Brother Vance for a long time. Then one day a letter arrived for my father. I read it alone in the tree house. It was from Brother Vance's daughter. She wondered if my father would collect Brother Vance's belongings from the root cellar and attic and ship them to her now that Brother Vance, like my mother, had passed on to his eternal reward.

There were not very many keepsakes. Everything fit in two cardboard boxes. The only thing my father did not include was the last misshapen parsnip preserved in the glass jar. He kept that for himself.

Father placed it on the bookshelf in his study where he could look at it when he gave me tutorials in scripture. He was quite the disciple now. He had the wearied look of a shipwrecked sailor, though he did his best to look cheerful. He often turned his chair facing the window where he seemed to be looking at the mailbox or the garden he had planted. He tended to it regularly, even if he was disappointed with the results. When he came inside with hands full of dirt he never washed them, always rubbing the dirt between his fingers until his hands were coarse.

Visitors from the neighborhood came to see father. They brought sympathy cards. They brought funeral potatoes and sparkling cider. He thanked them, but his mind was elsewhere.

Late in the afternoons father would shuffle to the mailbox and then return to his study where he examined cross-sections of vegetables under a microscope or pored over biblical verses. When I tried to capture his attention by playing the piano or showing him the drawings in *Weird Tales* he ignored me. "In just a minute," he would say, scribbling or muttering. "I'm almost finished."

Sometimes, while I waited for father to answer my questions, I gazed at the jar on the shelf. It seemed to be listening to us. Months—even years—later it showed no signs of decay. I could see the teeth marks where Brother Vance, or perhaps it was my father, had taken a bite and left it unfinished.

# Valdosta, After the Flood

Once we had a flood. It took only a few hours for the river to crest. The waters came through in a hurry making the roads impassable and disturbing the graves in the cemetery. Quite a few caskets washed down the streets. Some empty and others full. A few kids stood on top of the coffins pretending to surf. Other people used them as fishing boats. I watched the waters for a few hours from the porch. We were safe. We were on high ground. Then one coffin floated close to where the lawn used to be. A woman was inside using a broken plank of wood as a paddle. It was Grandmother. We had buried her a few weeks earlier. She looked about as ugly as you might expect from a buried grandmother. She paddled her way to dry ground, then stumbled up the grassy slope over the sandbags toward the house. Water dripped from her hair and burial gown. I took a long breath. It aimed to be a long evening.

She sat beside me on the porch in her old rocking chair. She said she was exhausted after all that paddling and such rain was giving her a headache and wasn't I going to offer her something to drink? She was parched. She was covered in a lot of mud, almost unrecognizable. But a boy always remembers his nana.

I pulled the hammer back on the pistol and placed it on the table between us. Just in case. I didn't offer her a towel.

I did offer her a glass of whiskey. She had worked up quite a sweat getting the coffin this far.

"Nana," I finally said, "I thought we agreed you would remain deceased."

Nana didn't say anything. She took little sips of whiskey. At the sound of my voice my wife came through the open doorway. "Is it thieves?" she asked, holding a baseball bat almost as big as her.

"No. It's no thief," I said calmly. "Just Nana."

My wife looked at me, perplexed as an old shoe. "What is she doing back? Isn't she dead?"

"That was the arrangement."

"Then what the hell is she doing here?"

"She won't say," I said. I looked over at Nana. Nana watched the flood. She hadn't been invited and didn't want to be impolite. My wife took a long look at Nana sitting on the porch having her sips of whiskey.

"If she won't talk then shoot her," my wife said.

Then she left us to fix supper.

"You look nice," Nana said once we were alone. "Not exactly happy, but nice."

"I'm very happy," I said.

"Are you, sweetie?"

I took a few sips of whiskey. I listened to the flood. It rippled. It murmured. The water in the street was turning more and more to mud. It was rising. If it kept up like this the high ground would get flooded. A crowd had gathered on the embankment to throw things into the flood. It was as if they weren't sure they would ever have another chance.

"I'd hug you," I told Nana, "but I just put on a clean shirt."

"It was niggers," Nana said suddenly. "They were looting graves. I thought it was the trumpets of the Lord calling me to my eternal reward but it was just niggers laughing. One minute we were there in our peace and quiet and the next we were floating away."

"No," I said, correcting her because I knew there was nothing she disliked more than being corrected. "We're having a flood. It's just one of those days when nature rears its ugly face."

"Whatever it is my dress is ruined," Nana said, flecking the mud off her hem.

She lit a cigarette. This was a new development, one I did not quite understand. The Nana I knew never smoked. Maybe this was not Nana? Her skin was pale, almost the color of lavender. She did not seem bothered by all the mud on her. This was also not like Nana. She was always one for cleanliness, a proper kind of Southern woman. She wiped her nose with the back of her wrist.

"You're not upset, are you, Nana?"

"Nope. I appreciate a good flood."

I could tell she was being polite. She was madder than a cat birthing a litter.

"You didn't leave us much choice," I started to explain, but then quit before trying.

The muddy waters pulsed and turned, coughing up all kinds of waste: a baby grand piano, clocks with no hands, a mattress, a record player with Leadbelly tunes, even a light bulb still clinging to the last of its glow. It all washed down the road in a patient ebb and flow.

"I wasn't dead," Nana insisted.

"In fairness, you weren't exactly living either."

We saw a few bodies floating in the water. Elderly or young we could not tell.

After a few hours we had suffered just about enough of Nana. She complained why had we buried her in such a terrible part of town where niggers rob graves. She complained that the man buried next to her smelled like a Jew. She tore down the curtains my wife put up because the color gave her a pain in the ocular zone, then hugged my wife and said it must be hard to keep a clean house with her condition, and told us if she was going to stay we would have to get rid of the pussy.

"I'm allergic to cats," Nana said.

"This is our house now. We inherited it," my wife said. "We can do with it what we want."

"What are you going to do with this big house, dear? You can't possibly use all the space."

"We want to start a family, Nana," my wife said.

"Oh dear, you're not going to nurse a baby with those tits, are you?"

While Nana was in the kitchen fixing the mess my wife had made of supper we stood in the parlor and spoke in low voices.

"Get rid of her. It's already a lousy anniversary," my wife said.

"She's family."

"We're trying to make a family, remember?"

I didn't want to argue. Her insistence on having a family frightened me.

"Can she at least stay for dinner? We can't send her away on an empty stomach."

I made up something about a new policy in the town bylaws. There is a twenty-four hour moratorium for the disposal of the recently deceased during floods, I told my wife. It was the law.

My wife took the pistol and aimed it on the lamp across the room. Before I could say anything she had shot out a window. It made a terrible noise, like a halo being ripped in half. That's the sound when a gun goes off—like a church bell calling after you.

"You have a choice to make. Get rid of her," my wife said as she handed me the pistol, "or I will."

She was serious. Once I had seen her crush three lady-bugs. Some of the parents at church had complained she told dirty jokes to the children in Sunday school. There was no telling what she was capable of, but getting rid of Nana was probably one of them.

It made me sad to think of what would happen next. When it floods we lose our wits. When it floods, we are no longer the person we see in the mirror. We have to be some-body else. When it floods there is no natural order, just the one we make with our hands.

"Come on, Nana," I said. "Help me throw these curtains into the flood."

Nana was happy to help. She took one bundle and I took another. We walked down the grassy slope onto the muddy embankment. I kept my eyes ahead of me on the gray stretch of neighborhood. It was that hour of night when the rain fell sad and nameless.

"This looks like a nice spot," Nana said.

"Just a little farther," I said.

We kept walking, careful not to slip in the mud. I asked Nana if she remembered the time right after my father died when I lost the lucky nickel he gave me. A bird had swallowed it at the park. And how my mom followed that bird for three miles into the swamp before she finally shot it with one of grandpa's pistols. But when we brought it home and cut it open we never found the lucky nickel. For a while every time we saw one of those birds we grabbed our slingshots until it got to the point we ran out of pebbles and the birds avoided our land. We had to let go.

"It was a pheasant. You don't soon forget something like that."

"Will you do me a favor? Will you tell my father I'm sorry I lost the nickel?"

"You can tell him soon enough, dear," Nana said. Even though I could no longer see her face, I knew she was smiling.

Then I hit her with the butt of the pistol. I did it gently. I didn't want to hurt her. She folded up like an accordion. It didn't take much effort to toss her into the flood. She floated for a few seconds, then drifted away.

I followed the mud back to the house. People on the other side of the flood were bringing out new sandbags. A few preachers were standing on the sandbags with outstretched hands, commanding the muddy waters in the name of Jesus to recede. The waters didn't listen. The waters rose. The mud thickened. Valdosta was going under.

A short ways from the house I saw a woman on the embankment holding a baby wrapped in a bed sheet. She turned in awkward circles. When she looked at me I could see she was crying.

"Have you seen my baby?" she shouted.

I eased myself down the mud bank. When I got closer I shook my head. "Sorry, lady. What did it look like?"

Without saying a word she pushed the bundle of sheets into my arms and jumped into the flood. I saw her bobbing in the waves for a second, this angelic and serene look on her face, and then she was gone.

When I pulled open the bed sheet it was filled with mud. Then I had the horrible feeling the woman had gone crazy and buried her child in the mud. I started searching for it, pulling back heavy mud slops into the flood water.

A man walked by with his teenage son. "Over here!" I screamed. They came running. I told them some woman lost her baby in the mud.

We pulled back heaps of mud. Pretty soon there was a crowd of people looking for the lost baby. Whenever somebody walked by, they wanted to help. It made you feel good about the world, especially on a day like this.

Some people were more serious than others. After an hour of looking I looked up and saw a few teenagers had begun to sculpt some of the mud into the shape of an enormous baby. They kept massaging handfuls of mud into the pile. People thought this was funny and strange and amusing. Pretty soon people stopped looking for the lost baby and took turns sculpting the mud baby. Nobody said anything. It was an awful silence. Too many people had lost something in the flood that now they were determined to find something, even if they had to make it out of mud.

"It's just mud," I said.

But they were having none of it. They brought more and more mud until the mud baby had a head and belly and big fat arms and big fat legs. It was huge. And it kept getting bigger. Now people were laughing. This was all just a game to them.

I ran away. I thought I was losing my mind.

My wife was waiting for me back at the house. She had a bath ready, which was good because I was covered in mud. She said supper would be ready soon.

"We're good people, right?" I said, putting my arm around her waist.

"Of course. We're happy, right?"

"Right," I said, but less sure than when I said it before.

I looked out the window. Not far away I could see the tower of mud taking shape. It looked like it might touch the sky, it looked like it would cover the town. Someday that mud baby would rise up and get rid of all of us. That's what happens after the flood. During the flood nothing makes sense. But after the flood—that's when the towering things emerge and make themselves known. It was just the nature of things. Just like sooner or later everything is replaceable and the young bury the old to make room for more young. We were not outside that circle.

I could hear the church bells, calling out far away.

I found the pheasant my wife had shot in the yard on the kitchen table. I cut it open and was not surprised when I didn't find my lucky nickel. I cut out its heart and watched it beat seventy-two times in my hand. Each beat sounded like a tolling bell that between beats liquefied with the rest of Valdosta.

# In Search of Fortunes Not Yet Lost

They had heard the rumors not to live beyond the prairie. This is Wynamucaquam, the townspeople told them. Ice storms, chopped wood, wild animals. Don't be anxious to tempt nature. Nobody lives at the end of a dirt road in a yawned space. It isn't forbidden, just abnormal.

Sully and Madeline couldn't distinguish between lies and the folksy caution of townspeople. They had come to Wynamucaquam with a fit of nostalgia. "Our relatives once lived here," they told the locals. The town had been settled centuries ago, a handful of miles before the Salagusa empties into Leech Lake. Most people never went east of the Erskine bluffs. The ones that did never were the same.

Sully was determined to come north. He wanted to walk in a field of snow and find only his footprints. He wanted to accidentally run out of firewood and have to smother himself in blankets. He wanted dead trees, icicles, dogs with thick fur, and frozen ponds. He wanted to grow a beard and look like a woodsman.

"Like in Snow White," his daughter Lorelei said.

He had to promise not to cut out anyone's heart.

They fell in love with a gingerbread Victorian on three acres of unfallowed parsnip fields with a barn full of what might have been horse bones. Unoccupied for twice a quarter century. It was nestled on the southern slope against a grove of trees that ran down the butte. Inside the Victorian were uneven floorboards. None of the doors closed. Only two of the windows weren't shattered.

"Not much privacy," Madeline said.

Sully grinned. "Privacy from what? We're in the middle of nowhere."

"That's what I'm worried about," she said, playing nervously with her hair as she often did when her husband started to daydream aloud.

He convinced her they could remodel the house themselves before winter. They would live off the land. Goats. Wild turkeys. Fishing. Old-timey stuff. The old man who sold them the property seemed amused by their expectations.

"Whatever you do," he said, "don't go believing you'll survive what nature offers. This town wasn't made for survival. It's a place of disappearances, not visitations."


At first they were afraid to meddle with the house and its ruin. Admire the front-facing gable. Little sips of sarsaparilla. Watch Lorelei get her head stuck between the balustrades and need a good buttering to wrench her loose. Three bottles of sarsaparilla. Gaze at cobwebs. Trot beside the wraparound porch with its warped stairs and rails. Hide-and-seek in closets. Cunnilingus at high noon while Lorelei was down at the pond. At night, watch a kaleidoscope moon through splintered glass windows.

For weeks they avoided the attic. It was only when Lorelei got lost that they discovered the roof had been damaged by the recent thunderstorms. Patches of sunlight and yesterday's rain dripped through hollowed-out spaces.

"You're not a handyman," said Madeline, tugging at his elbow. "Call someone."

"I know things. I can handle roofs."

"You've never been on a roof. You won't even climb trees."

But he was already pacing, his eyes fixed on the hollows, feet shuffling through broken shingles.

"I can fix it before winter. The stairwell, too."

She shook her head, knowing he had an infantile affection for decay.

"There's plenty you don't know about me," he said.

She knew him as the heir to a soda bottling factory. His grandfather had been a glassblower, his father a factory man and part-time soda jerk. On their wedding day, Sully received the first portion of his inheritance: one thousand cartons of fountain soda. Schwengers. A deranged sarsaparilla. The family brand. She had always suspected it was a joke. The factory had burnt, the estate auctioned, the collectibles dispersed. But the soda was part of the will and now that Sully had the house he was the proud owner of another thousand cartons. They kept the inheritance in the barn.

In bed Sully and Maddie laughed about living in a town where it seemed all the clocks had slowed. Like after they closed on the land and the paperwork had been signed they invited the old man to share a glass of sarsaparilla. They stood on the second floor open porch where in the distance Sully could see the smoke stacks of the abandoned distillery edge out from the tree line.

"What happened?" Sully asked.

"Town quit drinking," the lawyer said.

"You're kidding."

"There's a saying here: no need for liquor once you have a taste of winter."

"Are you lying or being serious?" Maddie sniggered.

He looked at her with an odd furl of his eyebrows. "What's the difference?"

The remodeling was not finished before the first snow. It was a light dusting, melting within three days, but enough to make them nervous. While Lorelei slept, Sully and Maddie hung canvas tarps blocking off the stairwell and upper floors. They would live together in the guest room through the winter. There was a single bed. They could huddle for warmth, he told her.

"We might freeze. If what people say is true."

"We have plenty of wood," Sully said, although he really had no idea.

A group of old women arrived that afternoon calling themselves a welcoming committee, but Maddie believed they were curious to see if the city people had survived the first snow. They brought the warm regards of the mayor. They were widows, mostly, except one housewife who was married to the grocer. Maddie invited them inside for coffee but they refused, insisting on introducing her to the local tea. Everyone in town drank the stuff.

For two hours the widows lectured Maddie. Too many middle-aged yuppies moving into town. People get ideas in a tired, cold place. They come to trudge barefoot through a nor'easter and think they can survive by pissing on their own feet, the kind of people amazed at rotted bones in an abandoned barn.

"Bunch of idiots," one of the women said.

"You've never seen a town so full of ice," said another.

"Yes, I hear the winters are brutal," Maddie smiled.

They corrected her: it was when the ice thawed that the

misery settled.

"Once winter comes you never want it to end," one of the widows said.

"Come April all you have are old wishes and empty bottles," another said.

"Change is the worst sort of thing in a place this far north," one of the fussy women said. "It's better if it just keeps snowing. You can leave things out in the snow and forget all about them. When the thaw comes, you have to remember everything. It's terrible."

Later, Maddie found Sully out in the field. She had tried not to laugh when he came home with an assortment of tools and soils and seed, along with the look on his face like a kitten unsure what to do with a dead bird.

"Don't you need a horse? Maybe a plow?"

"Shut up," he groaned. "I got hands. See? Old-fashioned," he said. "Half an acre to start. Nothing I can't handle."

"What about the roof?" she said.

He had stopped listening and was swinging a pickax.

She had tried to tell him nobody plants right before winter. He said the roots needed to freeze in order to maximize flavor. Don't worry, he knew. Seeds needed water, not snow, and what about sunlight? she asked. He said he'd go out each night and piss the half-acre wet if needed. Don't worry, he knew. He'd been reading books on parsnips, knew it so well he had even used the pages as kindling for the fires. By June they'd be swimming in parsnips. "This is the way my grandfather did it. I remember. Did I ever tell you about my grandfather's farm?" he said.

"You've been hearing too much about grandfathers."

"What does that mean?"

She walked back to the house, almost slipping on the porch steps thick with ice.

They lost Lorelei to a salt well. They found the window open and the bed empty and it was easy to follow the footprints in the fresh snow. They could only assume she had found a ladybug perched on the windowsill and followed it down the butte and into the thicket. Just that night at dinner she said she had made friends with one. "Ladybugs are good luck," Maddie said, half-smiling. "She must have gone looking for it."

People in town expressed sympathies. They all seemed to love the girl with the marigold hair.

Sully circled the well opening with some men from town. They lit crumbles of papier-mâché and let them float down into the blackness. When they squinted they could make out what looked like a little girl.

"Footprints end here," Sully said. He barely choked out the words.

"Won't do you any good to fish her out," said one of the graybeards. "Too risky."

"I want the body," Sully said. "It's my daughter."

The men all stuffed hands in their pockets and murmured.

"With the spring thaw the pressure from the brine pool causes the well water to rise. Frozen water on top, liquid brine beneath," one of the men lectured. "When it thaws she'll bubble right up without a scratch on her. She'll be fresh as the day she died."

"Isn't there something else we can do?" said Sully.

The graybeards shrugged.

"There's a chance she might rise up on her own. You'd be surprised," said one of the graybeards.

"Nobody in town will dig a grave in mid-January. Even

for a little girl with hair like that."

"Hmph," said one of the graybeards.

They were quiet. They smoked more cigarettes.

Sully first had the idea after finding the frozen bird. He had seen it outside Lorelei's window, completely still with its wings spread like it was trying to scare off a predator. The next day it was in exactly the same position. He climbed the tree and discovered it was frozen stiff. He boiled a large pot of water on the stove. When he dropped the bird inside, it sank to the bottom, then slowly rose to the surface.

He hefted the bucket of steaming water, hesitated, then began pouring it into the black skein of the well. He listened to the water crackling below. For a moment he wondered what would happen if he let himself fall. Would he just keep falling? Then he emptied the rest of the bucket. He did this nine more times. How many buckets would it take to make her rise? he wondered.

He did not tell Maddie. She wanted to be different now, for Lorelei's sake. No more out of the ordinary, she told him.

The town widows had come to invite her to join their association. They brought an assortment of pies and breads. Sully didn't want to offend them so he excused himself and trudged off into the woods. Maddie listened to these fussy little women correct her about her feelings and then declined to join with them. After all, she wasn't a widow. It would be best if she had some time alone.

"Best," one of the widows half-smiled.

"Thank you for your kindness," Maddie said. "But no, no thank you."

"No thank you, *please*," said another woman.

Maddie shut the door and sat in the darkness of the

house. She built a fire, then listened to the widows shuffle off the porch.

She went into Lorelei's room. Nothing had been touched since the accident. The princess dresses in the closet. Glitter on the carpet. Books at the foot of the bed. There was a brush on the nightstand with whorls of Lorelei's hair.

Maddie smashed the nightstand with her hand until one of the legs bent. Then she used her foot. She looked at her hand, waiting to see if it would bruise.

No thank you, please, the hand seemed to say.

In the distance she thought she heard Sully splitting a cord of wood. She found him half-dangled over Lorelei's well drinking a bottle of Schwengers. He dropped it, listening for the echoing splash.

"What's all this?" she said.

He dropped another bottle.

"Gravity," he said.


After two months she insisted he shave. She rummaged through the attic and found an old straight razor. First she steamed a towel and wrapped it around Sully's face. She opened and closed the old-fashioned straight edge razor. She was listening. For what, she wasn't quite sure only that it would be there when she least expected it. She flattened his cheek and pulled the razor over the skin. Maddie had never shaved a man before but she remembered spying on her father when she was four years old. She pulled the blade over the chin and it sounded like a door off its hinge, a door that had been slammed too often.

"You got out of bed last night," he said.

"I needed the fresh air. I wandered off the trail," she lied. "The snow caught me by surprise. I got lost. That seems to be going around."

His neck was a little bloody now. She was not being careful. He did not flinch.

"Tell me again the story you told Lorelei."

"I'd rather not," he said.

"Humor me. I'm holding the razor, remember?"

Once there was a girl with golden hair and silverslate eyes whose mother sent her into the forest to gather fruit to sell at the market. No matter where she looked she found berries and sweet roots and herbs, and her berries were never bitter, and her apples never too tart, and her figs never lost their flavor. And then during harvest morning the girl found two ladybugs huddled close on a fallen tree trunk. She watched them dance along the mossy bark. As she crept closer she realized it was a ladybug wedding. When they saw her the ladybugs made the girl with the silverslate eyes promise not to tell anyone their secret, reminding her that words are little sparks that can create large fires. The little girl tried to keep her promise but it was such a curiosity that she whispered to the aphids and the butterflies the secrets of the ladybugs, and no sooner had it happened that she wished she could turn back the clock, because when she stepped into the clearing she saw how lady luck had turned on her: the cornfields had been harvested and the stalks gathered and set on fire, only the farmhands had been careless with the matches and the winds had carried some embers to house and barn and her mother and sisters and her father and brothers had been burned into neat little piles of ash.

"It's just a stupid story," he said softly.

"You shouldn't have told her," Madeline said. "You should have kept your damn mouth shut, just this once."

Sully let her finish the shave. There was no sound in the kitchen except the razor on his skin. Hearing it made Maddie feel tired, like jam spread over too much bread.

She crawled into bed. She had waited until he left the barn before joining him inside the house. She must have woken him up with the sound of the ax but once outside he was distracted, not looking for her but hauling buckets back and forth. She had watched him. It didn't matter what he was doing. She didn't want to know his secret—she just wanted to keep him from hers. This is what happens in a place so far north.

"You frightened me," he said, as she tried to get comfortable in the bed.

He adjusted his pillow and put his arm around her. There were times before Lorelei had died when she felt him slip into the bed smelling of winter soil and she wanted to be naked next to him, like it was before, but there was no going back to how it was before, the life she once knew buried under a candied glaze of ice.

"I need to rest," she said.

It was strange to lie to him about something as insignificant as chopping wood. The idea came to her after smashing Lorelei's dresser. She liked the bruises that appeared, the way they purpled, then yellowed, so alien to what was normal. She liked how they took days to appear, making her alive with an ticipation. She held them up to the mirror. In a strange way, one she could not explain, the bruises helped her feel close to Lorelei whom she imagined white and bruised at the bottom of the icy well.

Madeline had taken the broken pieces of the dresser and dumped them in the well. She felt an immediate calm. She tossed more of Lorelei's things into the well each day, everything her husband had not put in a cardboard box in the shed. Then she had the idea to cut down trees. She would cut down the whole goddamn forest if it meant sealing off the well.

She had never handled an ax before and was worried she might slip and gash her thigh and have to crawl through the wood calling his name and he would mistake her for just another animal howl. Mostly she held the ax and never swung it: breathing the cold air, counting the seconds for her fingers to freeze, then her nose, wondering how Lorelei had lost feeling. Was it her legs that quit kicking? Did she know her screams had not reached out of the well? Tonight she had gotten the nerve to take a swing and found herself smashing bottles of sarsaparilla.

"Do you remember that time we ran barefoot through the snow?" she said.

He didn't answer. Maybe he was asleep. She reminded him anyway.

It was at the base of Mount Sugarloaf. What was the name of that shitty town? They had gotten lost looking for the Berkshires. That night he had dared her to go swimming across the Connecticut and if she froze to death he would keep her alive with his breaths until the sun came up. After they had both crossed he had told her to keep running to avoid freezing, the way animals survive a sudden cold. There was that moment when she stopped and he kept running, did he remember: left her behind while he ran with a wild screech and she was standing in the snow in the middle of nowhere, a young girl with this boy that she might love but wasn't sure, and she was naked as a peach and instead of freezing her toes began to burn. It was strange how something cold burns. She looked closely and saw she had scraped her toe. A little patch of red in the white snow. She decided then she wanted to marry him, to have a child made from their blood, a child who bled like them. It was a strange thing, naked in the snow, strange what the body does when it feels too much. It burns so that it doesn't have to feel at all. It was like nature slipping out and seeping inside all at once and not sure if you wanted more or less.

To anyone else the number of buckets would have been innumerable, but Sully never lost count. In a matter of weeks he had discovered how many steps from the back porch to the pump just beside the barn, from the barn to the stove where the buckets were heated, and then to the salt well. He knew how many seconds it would take. He knew how many drops of water would fill a bucket. His life was measured in numbers.

He wondered about his little girl's face, fearing that her eyes had become washy swirls of yellow, or that submerged so long strands of her hair would grow like wild weed along the well wall, or that the brine had pickled her. She wasn't quite dead though, was she? Not breathing but not rotting. Somewhere between.

He just wanted to see her hair one more time.

She was floating up. All those buckets of water. He was sure of it. In a few days he would be able to reach down and feel her. There was less splashing now, like the water was closer. He liked to tell himself it was only a question of time. There was plenty of that in the winter: time to think about time, to feel time, time to watch in the mirror as his body knelt to the wants of time, time to wonder if it was true what his mother had told him that when the day of judgment came the Lord would wake all his creations from the beginning to the end, a sudden rapture of dead things made fresh. As a boy she had told him that when God resurrected him he would know if he was going to heaven if the first thing he saw was a ladybug. They were the luckiest of all of God's creations.

Sully poured bucket nine thousand one hundred and eleven.

He fingered through the ice on the rim of the well, hoping to find a ladybug. There had been one the other night, during bucket eight thousand seven hundred forty-seven, and he had chased it through the wood. He swore it made this whirring noise, and while he knew it was crazy thinking, he listened for it now.

But the noise he heard was Maddie's ax thucking into the stump. He followed the sound until he found her. He watched her from the tree line. He had seen her doing this before, late at night, when she thought he was asleep. It was a waste. Didn't she know she might slip and leave a trail of her blood in the snow? Besides, there was plenty of firewood. What could she want with all this wood?

She knew he was watching but she kept swinging, following through the arc of her body and letting the ax handle slip down to the tips of her fingers. Let gravity do the work, she told herself. She steadied the next block and heaved. Soon she wouldn't be satisfied splitting wood from the forest. In a few days she would start dissecting the house: the floorboards, the walls, the stairwell, gutting it as if in search of the invisible weight that dragged her through her daily routine like a puppet on strings.

She paused to wipe the sweat from her face. Sully stepped from the edge of the trees fingering the patch of ice in his hands. He told her he was looking for ladybugs.

"Hmph," she said.

"Hmph," he said.

She kept splitting wood. Practice swings. She tried to sync herself with the falling snowflakes. Sully watched, wondering if in Wynamucaquam there was a natural rhythm of falling things.

# The Catapult of Tooele

The first exhibition of the catapult happened at the Tooele County Fair in 1901. The committee tried to create some mystique by saying it was an extraterrestrial gadget excavated from the Kennecott mine, and then a man from the academy said it had been left behind as a gift from the Goshute natives when the pioneers ran them off their lands, while anybody with common sense knew it was just some crazy Mormon with a couple of tools and plenty of screws loose trying to build a contraption capable of reuniting man with the heavens.

Lorenzo R. Snow, the Mormon prophet at the turn of the century, attempted to discourage the more zealous among his flock who had dreams of a modern-day Tower of Babel by turning the event into a farce and agreeing to preside over the catapult's virgin launch. He vaulted a sheep into Stansbury Bay.

It was quite the scene. Mormons from all across the state came to the fairgrounds to watch, because how many times are you going to see a prophet of the Lord catapulting livestock into the sky? Put that in the Bible and I guarantee you more people would read it and believe it.

There is a photograph in the *Tooele Transcript* commemorating Mormonism's first and only adventure in aerospace engineering. It is difficult to see the sheep floating away in the background, what with all the clouds in the sky and the hats being tossed in celebration. But it happened.

There are, of course, the usual skeptics. I've even heard people say the whole thing is a hoax and the picture is a forgery created by the Mormons with the help of J. Edgar Hoover. But I know better. A girl I used to date had a cousin who was friends with a polygamous family who read in their grandmother's journal that the sheep *was* launched only to reappear eleven months later, more than one hundred miles north in Tremonton, exhibiting no visible signs of trauma. They knew it was the same sheep because its ear had been tagged by the prophet himself. Under orders from the local bishop the animal was promptly roasted for the Sabbath meal.

The catapult remained in Stansbury Bay for about four decades where it acquired quite a reputation. Children used it to launch bad Christmas gifts and homework. Newlywed husbands reluctantly launched their collections of pornography. An entire shipment of a Coca-Cola truck disappeared thanks to the catapult. People were not spared. A congregation launched a dogmatic bishop. Boyfriends, girlfriends, teachers, union representatives, senators, and businessmen all suffered the ignominious fate. There is even a rumor that the mob launched Jimmy Hoffa in a pair of concrete shoes.

Then one day the catapult appeared in the marshes outside of Plain City. Its ropes were frayed and the nails holding the splintered wood in place were rusted by salted breeze. There had not been news of a launch in more than a decade. When I was growing up it was considered bad luck to touch the thing.

People say, well, that's a nice story, Red, but isn't it a little too much to believe? Isn't it a bit irrational to say the good people of the state of Utah were launching all their fears off some catapult into the bottom of the Great Salt Lake? Hmph, rational. Everyone untouched by the insanities of love still believes in reason.

Let me be clear. This is not some wackadoodle history. This is serious stuff. That nobody takes it seriously is hardly my fault. Not even my own daughter, my Lizzie—who had heard my stories about the catapult more than a hundred times, twice that if you count all the times I told it when she was in diapers—not even Lizzie took it seriously the night she joined the college boys on their way to Bear River Bay to launch a dozen chickens off the Catapult of Tooele. I tried to warn her. I told her if she went near that thing nothing would be the same. I tried to get her to stay home in front of the television and celebrate Ronald Reagan and the end of communism.

"It's Tom Brokaw," I said, turning up the volume. "He's your favorite reporter."

I watched old Tommy on the television as the Wall came down. He looked respectable in his hooded green coat and purple tie, his neatly combed hair, wearing gloves like some lumberjack and comforting us with that smooth voice that made you want to drink a bourbon without ice. He was just the man you wanted to tell you the world you know is ending and another one beginning.

For more years than I remember I have had a dream about meeting my dead wife. Men with headphones lead me out of the dressing room where I've been sprayed with cologne and given a bouquet of flowers. They've cut my hair and I look ten years younger. They push me through some curtains and into a room filled with bright lights and rolling applause. Tom Brokaw is the one to welcome me. He offers a rugged, Midwestern handshake and leads me over to the sofa where my wife is waiting. She is wearing a blue dress, blue as the sky, and is as beautiful as the day we married. We hug. We kiss. There are tears. I hug Tom Brokaw, too. A big man-hug that makes him chuckle with that Midwestern drawl. My dead wife and I start to catch up on lost times and old Tommy, turning to face the camera, gives the viewers at home a report of our love story in this brief moment in history.

I tried to get Lizzie to watch the Wall come down. Berlin suddenly looked like the place to be. People were dancing in the street. There was a clinking sound of hammers chipping away at the Wall. Other people perched on top of it with their hands in their pockets, like they didn't know what else to do but stand there and look surprised at what Reagan had made possible.

"It's a show for old people," Lizzie said, changing her earrings for the fifth time. "It's Thursday night. I'm going out."

"You'll regret it. Communism only ends once."

"But I need a boy who will love me forever," she said, kissing me on the cheek and racing out the door. She was like her mother—always quick with words. Not like me who stumbles to get a sentence out of his mouth.

So, she left me there in the quiet of our house. Suddenly, I did feel old. I felt old because I remembered when the Wall went up. I remembered thinking that behind that Wall the Russians would launch all kinds of Sputniks that would ruin this great country before I ever had a chance to get married and have children. That was the threat of communism—interfering with my nonexistent sex life. Now it was coming down and the naked truth was it did not happen the way I imagined. My dead wife was dead, and my little girl was off finding love. I felt old because suddenly I was one of those middle-aged men who believed a lot of things would happen only they never did. I wondered if Tom Brokaw had a daughter and if she took the night off to go out with friends, or if she was watching her father make history. I would never make history. Not even one of those faceless people in the crowd, tinkering away at the Wall, breaking off chips of history bit by bit. I was an antique, safe inside my own walls, whether I believed it or not.

I had to blame somebody for feeling the way I did so I blamed Grady. He had been around the house a few times. I had seen him and Lizzie talking in the driveway. It was easy to see she was smitten, but the boy, like most fools, was undecided about his feelings.

This business of launching the chickens with the catapult was Grady's idea. He was researching an article about the many wonders of Sanpete chickens and how they compared with the Vernal breed. Grady said the Vernal chickens were natural aviators. Lizzie said chickens don't fly. They were going to settle the matter once and for all.

They were almost ready for the first launch when Lizzie, always the adrenaline junkie, decided to place a bet.

"If that bird flies we'll get married one year from today," she said.

Grady looked at the Vernal chicken and then at Lizzie. They had known each other about two months.

"Done," he said.

Grady cranked the wheel until the rope went taut. Then he checked all the springs, making sure they were secure before a final inspection of the pivots and counterweights and barrel bucket tension.

The chicken screeched as it lifted into the evening sky. They lost sight of it in the fog, then shouted in disbelief as the wings unfolded, flapped twice, and the bird floated awkwardly toward Highway 83.

They launched six more Vernal chickens that night—two that plummeted into the lake, three aviators, and one that misfired into the sand and exploded on impact in a cloud of feathers. None of the Sanpete chickens even tried to fly.

Lizzie returned home late with the surviving chickens. They made a ruckus in the yard and sat at the back door clucking as if wanting to be let inside. I ignored them and watched Tom Brokaw assure us communism was dead and the world had less worries now than two hours and fifteen minutes earlier.

Before heading to bed Lizzie announced: "By the way, Dad, I'm getting married."

My dead wife liked to say that Lizzie had inherited her obnoxious habit of falling into things. It started as a little girl when she fell through the ice on the pond and almost died of hypothermia. I remember the look on her face in the hospital, with all the doctors and nurses wrapping her in special sheets and her poor mother a pale mess of tears. Lizzie's lips were blue but she smiled at it all in amazement, like she would jump in the pond all over again because the circus had come to town just for her. Later, she fell into ditches and wells and sand traps and got stuck in a number of places: boxes, drawers, cabinets, air ducts, industrial plumber pipe, and once at the top of the tallest tree in Box Elder County. We called the fire department so often they got to know her on a first name basis. When asked how it happened she would shrug and say she remembered falling but not much else.

After her mother died she had lots of boyfriends at school. She tried them out the way other people go through shoes. When she got tired of boys she took up a new job, and when a job got boring she found a boy to love for a while. She had a dozen jobs before she was eighteen: cake decorating, phlebotomy, fireworks design, even zymology, but eventually she fell in love with being a perruquierist. That's a wig-maker, for the uneducated. Her grandmother was excited because with so many wigs it was like she could have a different head for every day of the week.

The wedding was the first time I had ever seen Lizzie anxious to settle down. It was like she had fallen into things so often she figured this was as good a time as any to come to rest. Or maybe she just wanted to be a boil in my ass.

No, I did not approve of Grady. He was one of those intelligent idiots, a leftist who read a little Marx in a college class and felt the need to use fancy words like *bourgeois* or *dialectical unitarianism* and protest every damn thing in town. For a while Grady sold leaflets outside the Plain City rec center. For a nickel you could read all about class struggle and the exploitation happening at the Kuhni & Sons meat-packing plant down in Nephi. The boy was helpless.

Lizzie was quite pleased with herself that she had fallen in love with a radical. They got the funny idea that marriage is some social invention so it would be better if they didn't fall in love like normal people. Grady, who had graduated by then and was halfway across the world working for some newspaper, said what could be more romantic than writing love letters?

Grady's letters usually arrived on Wednesdays, so that became a kind of religious holiday in our home. Lizzie would primp herself all morning and emerge just as the mail boy made his delivery. The mail boy, who was more naive than intentional idiot, got wise to what was happening and started playing a joke with her every Wednesday, pretending there was never any mail for her. Nope, he would say, then watch her head back up the porch steps, all dolled up with those long legs of hers, and then suddenly he found the letter and she came over and thanked him with a kiss on the cheek. The boy was lucky she never killed him.

Lizzie read the letters with a sacramental silence. When she finished she tore them up and threw them in the fireplace.

"Well, that was something," she always said. What something? I wanted to know. Was it *something* he said? *Something* he did? *Something* he wanted? It's a terrible word, something. It ruins your mind with anticipation. But I was never invited into Lizzie's heart. It only had so much room and I knew she had always blamed me for her mother dying and turning me into an overprotective father.

I tried to pry out of her what plans Grady had for the future but she told me not to worry. He was flying over this country or the other, taking photographs of disasters and writing about the beauty of this thing we call living.

"Not many career prospects in beauty," I mumbled, trying to cast doubt in her mind.

"I don't see why you're so upset," she told me one afternoon. We had been out all day looking at cakes and ribbons and what color of trim to put on the wedding announcement cards. Now that we were home she was reading a stack of bridal magazines for the fiftieth time. The corpse of communism was not yet cold but somehow we had all overlooked the other great evil of our time: wedding planning. When the social history of wedding planning is written, my name will be buried in the footnotes as one of its many casualties.

"Can't you just be happy that I'm in love?" she said. "You're the one who said love is the only tyranny worth keeping, and all the other pinko ideas can get dumped on a deserted island with Jimmy Carter."

Just like a daughter to listen when you least expect it and turn your own words against you.

I said I had read the collected works of Moses Gomberg and Grady was not the kind of free radical you want to be exposed to. But there is no arguing with a young girl in love. They don't understand chemistry. Lizzie didn't understand that marriage is a lot like trying to fit an elephant into a shoebox—it's painful for both of you, no matter how much you laugh trying. It's like this granite temple they have in downtown Salt Lake. Pretty on the outside, but God only knows what's waiting on the inside. Marriage is a slippery sand that runs out between your fingers.

"That's okay," Lizzie said, ignoring the best wisdom I had to offer. "When I go to the beach there is nothing better than warm sand between my toes."

It came time for the wedding. The night before we had the awkward gathering of the two families. Grady's family didn't look like radicals. In fact, they seemed downright boring, all of them dressed in polo shirts and khakis like something out of a JCPenney commercial. Nobody said anything outrageous. Nobody got drunk and made a scene. Leonard Bernstein had died and the towel heads were blowing themselves up near the Holy Land, but nobody had connected the dots. Everyone was too busy laughing and eating Sanpete chicken. Everybody was in love with the idea of Grady and Lizzie in love, but nobody could see the writing on the wall.

The next morning, the morning of the wedding, there was a letter for Lizzie on the porch. It was from Grady. I found her on the couch in tears.

"Well, isn't that *something*. That sonfabitch," she said. "He got cold feet."

There is a pain that twists through you when you see your child in pain. I remember feeling it the first time Lizzie skinned her knee. We patched her up but she kept looking at her knee and then at us, as if to say, *Why did you let this happen?* It got worse as she grew older. There were no more skinned knees. Now it was bruised hearts and crushed dreams. We've erased polio and can swap out a human heart for a baboon one, but there is no cure for the pain I'm talking about. It is the pain of helplessness. It is the pain whose scientific name can only be *I told you so, why didn't you listen?* It is a naked pain. It starts small in the center and then radiates out, until it feels like a hot knife under your fingertips exploding into a thousand points of light.

Before I could put my arm around her she was out the door. "Nobody cancel anything," Lizzie said. "If I'm not back in an hour get rid of the priest and call a mortician."

She found him where we all knew she would—at Bear River Bay getting ready to launch himself on the catapult. It was a lousy escape plan. He had the wedding cake on his lap. He wore his tuxedo but was missing the shoes. He sat there with a hangdog look on his face, like he was both happy and ashamed he had been caught with his hand in the cookie jar.

Lizzie didn't scold him. She didn't cause a scene. In fact, she climbed into the barrel bucket and sat next to him. She held his hand.

"We'll do it together," she said, believing this was romance.

Before he could protest she had pulled the lever and launched the two of them.


At this point in the story people usually call me an idiot. Come on, Red, they say. You don't *really* mean they launched themselves from that catapult? That's just an urban legend. You can't *really* believe that, right? What you mean is the catapult is a metaphor for their broken engagement. What you mean is to corroborate the story that ran in the *Standard-Examiner* the next day saying more or less LOCAL GROOM DROWNS IN BEAR RIVER BAY. Nope. No, that is not what I mean at all. I am not a literary man. I metaphorize nothing. The drowning of a local groom and the grief of his heartbroken fiancée is a history too easy to be true. The *Standard-Examiner* says that what happened next never actually happened. True, I didn't see it. Nobody saw it except Lizzie and Grady. But if you believe in love you have to respect the absurd. And that is just what happened.

Lizzie launched them both. They were still holding hands two hundred feet over the lake when it became clear Lizzie was experiencing gravity in a different way than Grady. Lizzie was falling, but Grady was beginning to drift. When she splashed into the water—the cake followed a half-second later—he was rising head over heels in a kind of awkward flying, but mostly he tumbled higher and higher into the sky like a trapeze artist.

Why did she fall and he float? Why did he not take her with him? Well, communists make lousy husbands.

We arrived just as Lizzie swam back to shore. We helped her out of the water and she was pointing to where Grady was drifting in and out of the clouds. We tried to look but couldn't see him. She tried calling to him but it was no use. He was caught in the jet stream and seemed to have no plans of leaving it.

Lizzie stood knee-deep in the marshes for a few hours. She was still wearing the sopping wet wedding dress, her hand cupped to her eyes staring toward the sun. The girl did not blink.

"Well," she said, wriggling her toes in the sand. "That was *something*."

She did not say it then but I could tell she wished it had been her. I think she resented him, not for the embarrassment he caused, but because he hadn't done enough to take her with him. I grabbed her hand in mine.

"You got more sense than that," I told her. "You got the ground beneath your feet."

"Dad," she said. "Just this once I didn't want to fall."

There were various sightings of Grady throughout the years. Strangers from halfway across the world sent photographs to our house demanding authentication. He was spotted in the jet stream over Greenland and a suburb of Hattiesburg. Passengers on jumbo jets regularly claimed to have seen him floating about. At weddings all over the state, grooms and brides checked the skies before making their vows. During the peak summer marriage months, local weather reporting included a "Grady Forecast." There were at least a dozen instances of couples separating because one spouse or another saw Grady and took it as an ominous sign. Within a decade the Grady Clause became standard grounds for divorce. People were obsessed. Once we were walking the streets downtown and saw a woman wearing a T-shirt that said, *I ♥ Grady*. I wanted to punch her in the lip.

Lizzie received letters from all sorts of strangers. Quite a few were from delusional wives. My husband fell down a well and refuses to come out. My husband fell into his secretary's bed. My husband fell out of the window but I never pushed him. My husband fell into the gorilla exhibit at the zoo and went all reverse evolution. Some wrote to Lizzie asking what to do now that they had fallen out of love.

She told them all the same thing: go read a book on Marx. Love is a communist. It's the tyrant you can't live with or without.

At first Lizzie was sensitive to all these sightings. For the first few years she studied atmospheric charts from the National Weather Service. She visited all the towns in Europe they had agreed to see on their honeymoon. She crumpled up postcards and let them get blown away by the breeze, always hopeful one would find its way to Grady in the jet stream. It took a few years before she wasn't so sensitive to things floating in the sky. Oh, that's just a satellite burning up in the atmosphere, she said. It's just a small twin-engine plane. It's just a meteor shower.

It's easy to be unamazed. It happens to the best marriages.

On the five-year anniversary, a local millionaire sponsored an exhibition to see if it was scientifically possible for a man to launch himself into the jet stream. More than one hundred people signed up. Lizzie agreed to make an appearance. She told me she needed the closure, but I think she was hoping one of these other people would find Grady and pull him out of the sky.

One hundred and forty-two people. That's how many launched themselves into the Great Salt Lake. No casualties. No disappearances. All swam back uninjured. Nobody flew. Nobody floated into the jet stream. As a consolation prize for their contribution to science they received a plate of pit smoked lamb, compliments of a farmer from Tooele.

When it was just the two of us with the catapult I asked Lizzie if she had any thoughts on why things were different for Grady.

"It was a leap," she said. In that split second before their feet left the catapult bucket Grady leapt. "Maybe you have to want to fall as much as you want to fly," she said.

"It could have been worse," I said, doing my best to comfort her.

"Not likely."

"It could have been normal. He could have just drowned and there wouldn't be any hope."

Then she told me that life without Grady all these years was just that, a kind of drowning.

Lizzie married the idiot mail boy. Spencer or Albert, I think his name is. I've never learned it exactly. They live down the street. She kisses him goodbye each morning. He gets in his mail truck and delivers news of the world while she's Henny Penny waiting at home for something to fall out of the sky. I've seen the look on her face every day for ten years. She's never lost hope. She still believes one day her doorbell will ring and there will be a man in a tuxedo ripped to shreds with poufy hair blown back by the wind and a little bit of wedding cake on his lips. If walls can fall down why the hell can't a man float away in the jet stream? All the unbelievers can't seem to answer that.

Which brings me to last night. Get ready. Here it comes.

I was up late listening on the radio to SDI with Errol Bruce-Knapp. When you're a man with a heartsick daughter and a dead wife you have plenty of sleepless nights. Out of nowhere I had the urge to walk down to Bear River Bay in my pajamas where I found Lizzie sitting in the barrel bucket of the Catapult of Tooele.

It looked like some mythical creature there on the sand, worn away by years of rain and salted breeze. I wasn't sure if it would still work.

Lizzie was wearing her wedding dress. She looked pretty in a sad way. She didn't look at me. She focused on the lake, refusing to break her concentration, refusing even a glimpse out of the corner of her eye because in a situation like this so much depends on a glimpse. Looking this way or that is the difference between fact and fiction.

Without looking at me she said, "Are you going to ask me not to do it?"

"No," I said, thinking this was the first reasonable thing she had done in a long time. "But you should know you'll ruin the dress."

What else could I do? I cranked the wheel and inspected the pivots and counterweights. The sun was just coming up over the Wasatch Front. There was nothing left to say. We had exhausted all the words between us.

I looked over my shoulder to see if Tom Brokaw was coming through the marshes. This is one small moment in history he wouldn't want to miss.

I released the safety, pulled the lever, and let her go.

It sure wasn't flying and not quite falling. It was, well, it was something, something strange and something alien— and after that nothing was the same.

# Neophytes

No matter where I saw him, and there were at least a dozen different sightings that winter, the Saint pressed a butterscotch candy into my hand. The first few times it was the closest to magic I had ever been. I was singing a hymn in the church pew, or buying a package of nails at the hardware store with my father, when suddenly I felt the warmness in the center of my palm, like Jesus himself had been crucified there. I never cared for butterscotches, but now I was overwhelmed by the taste of a secret. I held it there on my tongue until the flavor dissolved. Maybe the third or fourth time after it happened my father, who was usually oblivious to such things, leaned close and whispered in my ear: "It was the Saint." I looked around but never saw any saint until one afternoon in January when we went out to Knob Hill to take photographs of the sun.

We climbed up a slope of dead grass, slipping on the half-melted ice, and stood with a few dozen other peepers whose heads twisted and craned to stare at that enormous egg yolk suspended in the sky. Dozens of cameras whirred. People huddled around photographs. Others stumbling with gauze pads taped to their eyes. Sun scramblers, Mother called them. People searching for something that wasn't there. Who the hell wastes a perfectly good Saturday like this? she muttered. My father ignored her, snapping a few pictures with a Polaroid. He gave one to my sister and one to me. "Be careful," he warned.

"You can see too much with too much light."

Mother stood with her arms folded across her chest, her eyes hidden behind oversized sunglasses. "Who talks like that?" she sneered.

"The Saint," father said without blinking.

Once the photo developed, my father asked if we could see it. See what? We were supposed to be looking? All I could see were blurs and smears of light. He pointed to the bands of radiating light. "There. It's a stairwell," he said.

I looked harder. Nope. It was a smear of light. I was wondering how many calluses I might need to walk up those stairs when I felt a tingling in my hand. A butterscotch. My body twisted left and right. The Saint was slipping through the crowd but paused to look at me looking. We stood there, unblinking, like when people stare at animals at the zoo and the animals stare back. He never spoke a word. Just tipped his old-fashioned hat with a sly grin and locked his eyes with mine as if to say, *I'll be watching.* And my eyes staring back and saying, *That's it?*

My father never thought of the Saint in any other way. "Sorry I'm late, *the Saint* needed some help fixing his fence," he would say. Or: "*The Saint* dropped by the office today." And: "You'll never believe what *the Saint* said tonight." It had been this way for years.

He was not a *real* Saint. Not the kind boiled in a vat of oil or flayed alive or fed to lions and somehow still wandering this good earth. One of his arms was withered but that was from a machinery accident. My father was aware of this, of course, but I think the distinction was lost on him. We knew very little about the Saint, other than what we heard in bits and pieces. He had plenty of money, fought in the war, wrote a book about Agatha of Sicily, and spent all his time caring for a sick wife.

It was the Saint who had inspired my father's curiosity in collecting. During the past year my father had amassed an entire closet full of junk. Nostalgic crap, my mother called it. Once or twice when he drove up the coast to see his brother or left for a weekend fishing trip—which my mother said was really an excuse to look for traces of God in bear shit—she would organize a yard sale. We took the money and bought greasy hamburgers which my father hated and said would give us heart disease. To heart disease! my mother cheered, toasting our plastic cups of soda.

A few days after returning from his excursions, gaunt and pale but optimistically dazed, my father hunted down his junk from neighbors and pawnshops and stored it safely in the closet until the next purge. The belief in the Saint was just one more thing my father couldn't bear to let go.

"Let's go see the Saint," my father said one night.

In the kitchen my mother broke a glass jar of pickled vegetables. That woman heard things not even owls could hear. I hesitated on the couch, listening to her sweep it up while my father stood near the front door holding a ceramic serving dish covered in tinfoil. Leftover pasta and meatballs. The Saint's favorite. His wife had been dying off and on for years and my father insisted on bringing a meal once a week. He needs us, he often told my mother. The Saint's wife had officially died the week before.

Mother helped with my scarf. She talked about the Saint being a fraud. Wackadoodle. Pervert. Words I couldn't repeat. To us he was and forever will be the Saint, but to her he was Roland Denny who lived in a loft above his shop that sold nothing but relics. In the encyclopedia next to the word *weird* she assured us we would find a picture of Roland Denny. "He believes *everything*," she warned.

We followed a country road into Old Town, crossing bridges into a thicket of trees whose greenness was almost black. The road snaked back and forth. During the drive my father explained how the Saint's wife had suffered from a terrible illness for almost two decades. Not even he could pronounce it. Now that she was dead it was likely the Saint would sell the shop and move elsewhere, maybe back east where he had been born. We might never see him again.

"Such a brilliant man," my father sighed.

I said nothing. I didn't feel old enough to be joining him, much less learning about any of this. Just nodded my head with a mixture of fascination and disbelief.

The dim lights of Old Town lay ahead. There were still a few shops on Main Street, but otherwise this part of town had been abandoned. At one time it was the center of life in our city, but now it was just sad. Things die and nothing takes their place.

A few years earlier a girl had gone missing in Old Town. We all worried it was the Coal Creek Killer again. Teams of specialists with dogs searched the nearby woods. There were vigils. Her face was on the news. The girl's parents prayed for her safe return. One morning they found a liver wrapped in a sweatshirt nailed to a tree. There was a note scribbled in blood. Then about ten feet of tripe washed up in a nearby creek. My sister and I were not allowed to walk to school by ourselves. My parents wouldn't even let us leave the window open at night. Then the girl just walked out of the woods one day. It was all a hoax. She had run away with her boyfriend and the two of them stole some pig guts from the high school biology lab as a joke. A lot of people were upset, but I couldn't tell if it was because they were disappointed the girl wasn't dead or if for the first time they realized how easy they could be played for fools.

In a strange way my father's invitation felt like a hoax. Like he was trying to make it more magical and ominous than it really was so years from now we could recall it with a certain fondness. "Remember that night when we saw the Saint?" he would say. That kind of fatherly crap.

The car stopped in front of a shop on Main Street. Darkened display windows gazed back like empty eye sockets. We sat there with the engine idling.

"This is it," my father said.

Disappointment swelled, compressing my heart like a sponge. It was an old brick building sandwiched between dozens of other old brick buildings. It did not appear like the house of a Saint. I'm not sure what I was expecting, but I wanted it to look different. I wanted the Saint's shop to be strange or frightening with a certain look of ruin. Standing in the street it felt like any other aged shop in an aging part of the world.

It was only coming closer that I felt differently. I could not imagine why any decent human being would want to live here. It was cold. It was quiet. The road behind us now seemed far away. A dense web of trees and vegetation loomed behind the buildings, all of it covered in a silvery shade of frost. Something was in those trees, something that sensed a disruption in the natural rhythms of this place, but I had no idea what. I had spent all last summer standing by the wood near our house, disappointed I never saw a coyote. "Just because you didn't see it," my father said, "doesn't mean it didn't see you." That's how I felt walking toward the Saint's shop. Coyote eyes drinking us up.

"It's lovely, isn't it?" my father said, breathing deeply as if the air was somehow purer than what he breathed in every night in our yard. "Wouldn't you like a place like this to call home? A place all to yourself."

"Yeah," I said.

"He likes his privacy. He's not used to visitors," my father said. "Strangers bother him."

"What about you?"

"I'm not a stranger."

"I guess."

We stood there waiting.

"Try not to ask too many questions. And don't touch anything."

"Why not?"

My father shrugged and his face twisted.


When I had seen the Saint in the crowd of sunlight peepers on Knob Hill I had not *really* seen him. It was only a glimpse. There had been something angelic about how he moved through the crowd, almost like he could move without being seen. Then before I had time to think about it he was gone. It was the same Saint standing behind the glass display case, but not what I was expecting. I had never realized how much older he was than my father, his hair more gray and frazzled than I remembered. His shoes were too big. He fidgeted with the ring on his finger, taking it off and on. Looped around his belt was a thick lock of braided hair, maybe taken from a wild animal. I kept looking for that mischievous expression, or any gesture of affection, but he was more somber now. Nothing about him shied away from the pain he was feeling.

I don't remember what kind of shop it was exactly. Rare books, antiques, maybe. I'm probably remembering this all wrong and the man was just a pawnbroker.

The Saint accepted the ceramic dish of meatballs and set it on the display counter. He pushed a glass of water into my hand and poured a shot of liquor for my father. My father accepted this graciously but did not drink. The metallic taste of the water tickled the insides of my ears with each swallow.

All of a sudden the Saint clapped his hands and rushed through a curtain into a back room. We followed through a narrow hallway until we were standing in a small library. Bookshelves stretched from floor to ceiling. Such an overwhelming musty stench. Admiring the books, I almost tripped on the assortment of floor rugs. My head spun trying to follow the arabesque pattern of one, and my body felt warm and silly gazing at another with its grotesque figurines of naked men and women conjoined together. My father stood over one of the figures, covering up as much of the scene as possible with his feet, his face flushed with embarrassment as the Saint handed him a book and continued his previous conversation in a low voice. It didn't concern me, the whispers of one old man to an even older man, each with one foot in the grave of the past.

On the far side of the room, spread against a wall adjacent to the only window in the room, was an enormous map of the world. Thumb-tacked to this map were photographs and little drawings. Different colored strings connected the tack on one city or country to another, creating an elaborate web.

"What's this?"

"These are things I know exist but have not yet seen," the Saint said.

There was a sketch of a unicorn on a napkin. A photograph of a UFO. A woman blowing out the candles of a birthday cake. A single flower growing on a cliff overlooking the ocean.

"Come," the Saint said with a smile, "I'll show you something even better."

A light flickered on in the hallway and we squeezed past a towering stack of dehydrated apples in tin drums. Even though the hallway appeared to be level I could feel the walls on either side closing in and narrowing to a point that seemed farther and farther out of reach. I couldn't believe this was all part of the same building. My chest was tight. I kept glancing behind me at my father, wondering if he would put an end to this derangement, but he smiled weakly in affirmation that we were safe. At least for now.

The Saint walked beside me. The only Saint I'd ever seen before was in paintings in school books or sculptures in a cathedral. Those saints had agonized faces and loose, flowing robes. Halos or something. They were men with beards. I remember seeing postcards of my parents' trip to Italy one summer. There was a sculpture of Saint Bartholomew who had been flayed alive. He wore his skin draped around his neck and shoulders like a fashion accessory. My father spent hours explaining every detail of the sculpture and how the man who carved it had robbed graves and dissected the bodies. What amazed me most in the sculpture was the chiseled abs. In a creepy way it made you wish you could lose your skin because then God would transform you into a superhero.

The Saint was nothing like this. He was flabby. He did not wear a robe. He did not have a golden halo floating above his head. He lacked celestial charm. In fact, the sight of him was downright ugly. For the first time I saw the hand withered from the machinery accident, suddenly disappointed it was not more mangled. His nose was a fat, bulbous pickle at the end of his face, tinted slightly purple with veins. He looked like a clown.

We moved slowly down stairs and into a cellar. A womb of darkness pulsated around us. It smelled earthy. The air was chilly, or at least I allowed myself to imagine it was. A hand clamped down on my shoulder in the darkness. I let out a small yelp, but then the fingers on the hand pinched my shoulder gently and I knew it was my father.

A single halogen bulb illuminated a small corner in the room. We watched as the Saint slipped away from under the bulb and shuffled into the darkness. Above us, the ceiling was unfinished, exposing a network of pipes and wires and beams. A single drop of water splashed on my cheek. Another halogen bulb flickered on ten feet away. Again, the Saint disappeared into the darkness. Coming down the stairs I had believed we were in a tiny cellar but with each successive halogen bulb I realized the error of my thinking. It took the Saint a full minute to walk across the concrete slab back to us.

My eyes adjusted to the light. Now that I wasn't squinting I saw along the walls of the cellar a series of cabinets with glass doors. The Saint led me forward. Through one glass pane I saw a leather strap with a rusted buckle. Between the buckle was a double-pronged fork. A heretic fork, the Saint explained. He removed it from the cabinet and displayed how the fork would be adjusted just under the chin so that any movement would cause the sharpened prongs to pierce the skin. My fingertip pressed the fork tip. It was like clasping hands with the past.

The Saint gave me a detailed history lesson on every item in his collection. There was an assortment of thumb-screws. A long claw heated and clamped to a woman's breast. The Spanish Spider, the Saint said with a wheezing chuckle. There were more common items—an ax, a doubled-handed saw—but the Saint seemed to relish the more bizarre instruments of torture whose descriptions rolled off his tongue like poetry. Intestinal crank ("Somewhere between nine and thirteen feet of small intestine could be removed before the victim perished."). Crocodile shears ("For snipping and tearing, or simple mutilation."). Vials of oil mixed with beef tallow that had hardened into a kind of soap ("Remains of Margaret Davy. Boiled. 1542."). Some frayed rope ("Anne Askew. The rack. 1546."). A set of rusted iron rings with chain links connecting to metal bracelets.

"I have yet to associate a name with this artifact," the Saint said, obviously troubled. He cleared his throat. "The victim would have been fastened to the chains and the chains fastened to horses that pulled in different directions. Sixteenth century, I believe."

The Saint placed in my hands another contraption shaped like a metallic pear. When he turned a key-handle the four leaves of the device slowly opened. The Saint opened and closed the instrument several times. Flakes of metal danced to the floor.

"They called it the Pear of Anguish. This would be inserted into the victim before application."

I did not ask where the device would be inserted. I'm not sure I wanted to know.

We kept moving slowly to the other end of the cellar.

I tried to remember every item, every minute detail, not so much to catch him in a mistake, or tell my friends later, as to wait for a chance to ask the question eating a hole in my mind: are you *really* a Saint? I didn't want to play the part of heretic. Not here. Then other questions suspended in the jelly of my mind: is this what saints *do*? With every torture device pressed in my hands I couldn't tell if the Saint was being serious or indulging my imagination. It seemed impossible for anybody to know so much about such odd things. There were just things. Old things. But somehow they felt more alive than us. Waiting. Full of anticipation. Once or twice I glanced behind at my father who stood with his eyes closed as the Saint discussed a tongue suspended in a jar of formaldehyde, nodding gently as if he had heard the Saint recite this sermon a hundred times before.

It was easy to see the Saint frequented this cellar often. He was very comfortable here. His voice was different. Everything had been expertly arranged, the glass neatly polished for our arrival. What I could not decide was why this place existed. Was it a kind of self-inflicted punishment? Or did it please him? Was he a monster? Or perhaps it was something else. Maybe thinking about the pain brought him closer to God. Maybe the Saint was still trying to figure out why any of this existed, why we would exist to make such things, and someday, maybe, after enough living in its presence he would have the answer.

In a far corner, away from the other relics, was the inquisitor's chair. The jagged spikes had been expertly polished. Without saying a word the Saint nudged me to take a seat. He grinned. I looked back at my father who shrugged and chewed the insides of his cheeks, his mouth twisting into a playful smile. Without warning, the Saint lifted me onto the chair. Immediately, I felt the spikes press against my skin through my clothes. It pinched. I swallowed hard. The Saint explained that witches were clamped into the chair with iron braces which could be tightened to further compress the victim into the iron spikes.

"There's no such thing as witches," I said quietly.

The Saint pretended not to hear me. He was assuring my father all these relics had been authenticated. Nothing was fake.

"How can you tell the difference?"

The Saint let out a long breath. He knew the answer to this, probably rehearsed it for everybody he brought down into this private hell, but was reluctant to say or merely searching for the right words.

"There are ways to trace ownership," he lectured. "Documents and such. And more scientific methods. But, the only real way to know is to use them."

We climbed the stairs. I felt very heavy, almost as if I was wearing old-fashioned diving gear with weighted boots. Thoughts danced wildly in my head as we left behind the Saint's little underground museum. What would be most painful: being sawed in half, having a rat burrow into your chest, or slowly disemboweled? I would not want to be flayed alive. That took time and imagination. Maybe there was something worse, something not yet imagined. I didn't think it was possible people still invented this kind of stuff, but I guess as long as there were people we would need the things in the Saint's collection. By the time I reached the top of the stairs I had changed my mind. I looked at my fingernails. I liked to chew on them. They were always bleeding. The whole time we were in the cellar I had gnawed on them unwittingly. I tried to remember what the Saint had said when he pointed out a pair of pliers. Sometimes the nails were peeled away, slowly, while other times a splinter or iron wedge was pressed under the nail, slowly, then expertly driven with a mallet to crumble the joints.

"The smallest things yield the worst agonies," the Saint had said.

Instead of turning left down the hallway with the tins of dehydrated apples back towards the main room of the shop, we took another staircase leading to the loft.

"Roland," my father said quietly. It was the first time I had ever heard him speak the Saint's name. "Roland, please."

But the Saint did not listen. Passing through the loft we reached another door. The Saint removed a set of keys from his pocket. "This is my wife's bedroom," he said.

Things die. Old things. Young things. Something dies every day. A woman down the street put her head in the oven. A father blew up too many balloons for a birthday party and dropped dead of a heart attack. The neighbor with the pet snake was strangled in the night when it escaped the cage. A Ferris wheel at the county fair toppled, killing seven. During a sandstorm, a couple married for fifty-two years suffocated on the air they were breathing. Just last week when I left for school I saw a pigeon fly right into the upstairs window. It just lay there in the broken glass until my father scooped it up with the shovel. After school I looked in the trash can. The pigeon was still there, teeming with flies. I knew this. But nothing prepares you for stepping into a room where a real person died.

It was poorly lit. There was a dresser and antique writing desk. Along the edges of the floor, pressed close to the wall, were unlit candles. Exquisite care had been taken to make the bed. Unwrinkled sheets. Fluffed pillows. Beside the bed, on the other side of the nightstand, was an armchair. I could see the imprint of the Saint's butt on the cushion. That's the Saint's butt, I thought. A holy, menacing butt.

The Saint said his wife had spent the last fourteen years of her life in this room. Right there, on that bed, he whispered. This is where she wanted to be.

"Fourteen years," he said, his voice crackling. I tried to picture the Saint's wife in that bed. I doubt she ever left it. She couldn't have. She must have known about the cellar. She probably helped him collect all that stuff. I mean, she was his wife. How else do you stay married unless you really know somebody? Maybe her illness came from this place, those things lingering beneath her the way an iceberg hides beneath the water. Knowing that museum existed but not knowing why it existed, not knowing what she had married thirty-seven years before. Man. Fourteen years in that bed. She had all the torture she needed right here. It's impossible to really know anybody.

Reaching into the nightstand the Saint handed me several photographs. I recognized them. They were photographs of the sun. He mentioned how during the winter his wife liked to stare at these for hours and in the summer she would open the blinds and stare at the sun until her eyes throbbed. Next he handed me a glass jar with what looked like an oversized bean. This was the toe of the missionary Andrzej Bobola, bitten off from the corpse after his torture by a devout follower. He had other relics. A rose petal transfigured from the corpse of Catherine of Siena, and a vial of breast milk from Saint Agatha.

"Preservatives," the Saint said.

Nothing else worked. Not the herbal diets, the pills, the oils, the balms—not the radiations, the operations, the experimental drug trials. No, the Saint said, his voice now in a dream, those were a lost cause. It was these, he said, motioning to the relics. He had kept these close to his dying wife, sometimes hiding them under the pillow or putting it in her hand while she slept. It was the relics, the Saint said, that had sustained her, *preserved* her, through fourteen years of suffering.

"She was a saint," the Saint said. His fingers rubbed the lock of braided hair looped around his belt. "You should have seen her when it happened."

Before leaving, the Saint showed us one last glass container. The object inside looked like a shriveled banana peel. He called it the Holy Prepuce. Jesus's foreskin. The only thing that did not ascend with the savior of the world into heaven, although the Saint suggested that some early theologians believed the foreskin was taken from this earth to form the rings of Saturn.

"Had it touched my wife's lips this would have healed her," the Saint said.

"Too bad you didn't have it before she died," I said.

"Simon!" my father hissed.

"No, I did," the Saint said with an uneasy smile. "I've had it for years."

I held the relics. I held that holiness. I wish I could say they felt different from the pliers or the pear of anguish, but that's not the way I remember it.


Using the Polaroid, my father took a picture of me with the Saint outside the shop. Then we shook hands. His touch was strange. Like I could grasp his soul but not the body. Touch without touch. It was weird. My father handed the photograph to me as we walked back to the car. I stuffed it in my pocket. Behind us, the Saint waved.

"You shouldn't believe everything he says," my father whispered. It felt like he was floating away and somehow I was keeping him tethered to the ground.

"It's fake? All that stuff is fake?"

The car backed into the street, the brakes screeching like two banshees in a secret conversation.

"No. No, it's real," my father said with a measured hesitancy, "it just isn't true."

He said this twice. Almost like he wasn't sure whether the words were actually his own. I felt in my pocket for the photograph but instead discovered a butterscotch candy. It looked like a lost orb of sunlight. I put it in my mouth so I didn't have to say anything else.

As we helped set the table I told my mom and sister all the things I had seen. My sister didn't believe me. My mother was very quiet until I came to the part about the Saint's dead wife and the Holy Prepuce and my mother said she could only imagine the misery and torture the Saint had inflicted on that poor woman, keeping her alive all those years for a miracle cure that never came.

"I would do nothing less for you," my father said. "I love you too."

We ate leftover pickled cabbage. Mother kept her eyes open during the prayer. Big coyote eyes. Inquisitive. Elsewhere. Staring out the window. Scrambling for the sun in all that night. My father's words had knocked the wind out of her. The color had drained from her face, too. She would look at him like that for years to come, much quieter than before, as if curiosity had a strangle on her. I closed my eyes and imagined all the relics I would touch next time I went to see the Saint, praying they would wait for me and not forget my touch. My father kept praying and thanking God for all the creeping things in the world, and I suppose that meant the Saint and his dead wife, and all the people and saints who had gone before us who made it possible we could have thumbscrews and intestinal cranks and foreskins, and all the other things real and not true that leave us aching with imagination.

# Acknowledgments

Grateful acknowledgment is made to the following publications in which these stories first appeared, sometimes in slightly altered form:

*Los Angeles Review*: "A Cosmonaut's Guide to Microgravitic Reproduction";
*Bat City Review*: "A Genealogical Approach to My Father's Ass";
*Chattahoochee Review*: "An Unfinished Man";
*Carolina Quarterly*: "Ellie's Brood";
*Cream City Review*: "Everything You Wanted to Know About Astrophysics but Were Too Afraid to Ask";
*Cincinnati Review*: "Frustrations of a Coyote";
*Hotel Amerika*: "Indulgences";
*Mid-American Review*: "In Search of Fortunes Not Yet Lost";
*Four Chambers*: "The Catapult of Tooele";
*Red Cedar Review*: "The Fertile Yellow";
*Phoebe*: "The Foot";
*Fiction International*: "The Good Nazi Karl Schmidt";
*Tusculum Review*: "Valdosta, After the Flood" (originally as "Valdosta, Left to Ash");
*The Fourth River*: "Veyo, Forgotten by the Mormons";
*Bitter Oleander*: "Visitation";
*Dislocate*: "What the Body Does When It Doesn't Know What Else to Do";
*Burrow Press Review*: "Your Tragedy Is Important to Us."

❖

It took thirteen years for this book to come together and in that time I have enjoyed a vast support system from various friends, colleagues and mentors.

It would not have been possible without the following individuals: Sam Michel, Peggy Woods, Speer Morgan, and Marly Swick—your artistic insights made these stories better. To a few teachers in particular I owe a debt of gratitude: Margaret Young, who believed in my work when I had no idea what I was doing; John Bennion, who didn't flinch at my impulsive weirdness and taught me to follow my instincts; Chris Bachelder, who took me back to the basics and encouraged me to write the kinds of stories I wanted to write; Kate Bernheimer, whose fairy-tale workshop was nothing short of miraculous; Trudy Lewis, who taught me the art of restraint; and Karen Russell, whose enthusiasm for my work was infectious.

To my workshop peers in the Creative Writing Programs at UMass Amherst and the University of Missouri— thank you for suffering through early incarnations of these stories. The generosity of your feedback is nothing short of remarkable.

I give a special thanks to Aaron Hellem for poring over manuscripts at the Amherst Brewing Company as we subsisted on jalapeño poppers and fried pickles, believing we were our own lost generation.

Thank you to Peter Conners, Ron Martin-Dent, Daphne Morrissey, and all the good people at BOA Editions for their editorial guidance and aesthetic vision, but most of all for believing in this manuscript and giving it such a wonderful home.

To the editors of the magazines and journals where these stories first appeared—thank you for giving me a chance. To the editors who rejected these stories for one reason or another—you did me an incredible favor: there is little motivation quite like a rejection slip.

Neither would this book be possible without my family.

To my somewhat puritanical extended family who might read this—my apologies when these tales invariably offend you, but to censor the imagination is a terrible thing. Thanks to my mother, who taught me the joy of escaping into books. To my father, a master of exaggeration. To my brothers, for their witty banter. To my children, whose weirdness makes me want to turn back the clock.

And above all, to my wife, Jenna, who spent innumerable hours listening to me ramble through these stories and rolled her eyes and shook her head but always believed my work mattered. You are the only one who truly understands me.

## About the Author

Ryan Habermeyer was born and raised outside of Los Angeles. He earned his MFA from the Program for Poets & Writers at the University of Massachusetts, and PhD from the University of Missouri. As a scholar of European folklore and fairy-tales he has lectured nationally and internationally on the genre. He lives with his wife and children on the Eastern Shore of Maryland where he is Assistant Professor of Creative Writing at Salisbury University.

# BOA Editions, Ltd. American Reader Series

No. 1   *Christmas at the Four Corners of the Earth*
Prose by Blaise Cendrars
Translated by Bertrand Mathieu

No. 2   *Pig Notes & Dumb Music: Prose on Poetry*
By William Heyen

No. 3   *After-Images: Autobiographical Sketches*
By W. D. Snodgrass

No. 4   *Walking Light: Memoirs and Essays on Poetry*
By Stephen Dunn

No. 5   *To Sound Like Yourself: Essays on Poetry*
By W. D. Snodgrass

No. 6   *You Alone Are Real to Me: Remembering Rainer Maria Rilke*
By Lou Andreas-Salomé

No. 7   *Breaking the Alabaster Jar: Conversations with Li-Young Lee*
Edited by Earl G. Ingersoll

No. 8   *I Carry A Hammer In My Pocket For Occasions Such As These*
By Anthony Tognazzini

No. 9   *Unlucky Lucky Days*
By Daniel Grandbois

No. 10   *Glass Grapes and Other Stories*
By Martha Ronk

No. 11   *Meat Eaters & Plant Eaters*
By Jessica Treat

No. 12   *On the Winding Stair*
By Joanna Howard

No. 13   *Cradle Book*
By Craig Morgan Teicher

No. 14   *In the Time of the Girls*
By Anne Germanacos

No. 15   *This New and Poisonous Air*
By Adam McOmber

No. 16    *To Assume a Pleasing Shape*
          By Joseph Salvatore

No. 17    *The Innocent Party*
          By Aimee Parkison

No. 18    *Passwords Primeval: 20 American Poets in Their Own Words*
          Interviews by Tony Leuzzi

No. 19    *The Era of Not Quite*
          By Douglas Watson

No. 20    *The Winged Seed: A Remembrance*
          By Li-Young Lee

No. 21    *Jewelry Box: A Collection of Histories*
          By Aurelie Sheehan

No. 22    *The Tao of Humiliation*
          By Lee Upton

No. 23    *Bridge*
          By Robert Thomas

No. 24    *Reptile House*
          By Robin McLean

No. 25    *The Education of a Poker Player*
          James McManus

No. 26    *Remarkable*
          By Dinah Cox

No. 27    *Gravity Changes*
          By Zach Powers

No. 28    *My House Gathers Desires*
          By Adam McOmber

No. 29    *An Orchard in the Street*
          By Reginald Gibbons

No. 30    *The Science of Lost Futures*
          By Ryan Habermeyer

# Colophon

BOA Editions, Ltd., a not-for-profit publisher of poetry and other literary works, fosters readership and appreciation of contemporary literature. By identifying, cultivating, and publishing both new and established poets and selecting authors of unique literary talent, BOA brings high-quality literature to the public. Support for this effort comes from the sale of its publications, grant funding, and private donations.

❖

*The publication of this book is made possible, in part, by the special support of the following individuals:*

Anonymous
June C. Baker
Angela Bonazinga & Catherine Lewis
Dr. James & Ann Burk, *in memory of Morrison*
Chris & DeAnna Cebula
Art & Pam Hatton
Jack & Gail Langerak
Melanie & Ron Martin-Dent
Joe McElveney
Boo Poulin
Deborah Ronnen & Sherman Levey
Steven O. Russell & Phyllis Rifkin-Russell
Sue S. Stewart, *in memory of Stephen L. Raymond*